ECHOES OF THE PAST

BY

KERRY BRACKETT

Dedicated to my grandmother who always supported me, no matter what I decided to do in life. Love you!

Table of Contents

Chapter 1

Arrival at Twilight

As the sun began its descent, painting the sky in hues of crimson and gold, James and Nikki's car rolled into the small town of Ravenswood. The town, nestled deep in the heart of the countryside, was a place neither of them had heard of until their recent research into forgotten histories led them here. The goal of their journey was to uncover stories lost to time, and Ravenswood, with its mysterious past, seemed like a promising starting point.

The road leading into town was flanked by dense woods, their shadows growing long and twisted in the twilight. The air was thick with an expectant silence, broken only by the rhythmic crunch of gravel beneath the car's tires. James glanced at Nikki, who was focused on the road ahead, her eyes narrowing slightly as she peered through the windshield.

"Feels a bit like stepping into a different world, doesn't it?" James mused, breaking the silence.

Nikki nodded, her lips curling into a slight smile. "It does. There's something… timeless about this place."

As they drove further into the town, the first signs of life appeared. Quaint houses lined the street, their facades worn but charming in their antiquity. Each home seemed to whisper stories of generations past, of lives lived in quiet obscurity. Yet, there was an undeniable air of neglect; paint peeled from wooden shutters, and the gardens were overgrown with weeds that swayed gently in the evening breeze.

The center of Ravenswood revealed itself to be a humble square, dominated by a stone fountain that had long since run dry. Around it stood a cluster of small businesses—a diner, a hardware store, and a general store with a faded sign swaying gently in the breeze. A few locals milled about, their faces etched with lines of time and experiences unknown to outsiders.

James and Nikki parked their car near the diner, eager to stretch their legs and perhaps gather their first impressions of the town. As they stepped out, the cool evening air wrapped around them, carrying with it the faint scent of earth and something else—something indefinable yet unmistakably ancient.

Inside the diner, the atmosphere was subdued. A handful of patrons sat scattered among the booths, quietly sipping coffee or picking at their meals. The clinking of cutlery and the low hum of conversation were the only sounds that filled the space. James and Nikki chose a booth by the window, offering them a view of the square as dusk settled in.

A waitress approached, her eyes tired but friendly. "Evening, folks. What can I get for you?"

Nikki glanced at the menu before ordering a coffee, while James opted for a slice of pie. As the waitress left, Nikki leaned across the table, her voice a conspiratorial whisper. "Do you feel it? That... atmosphere?"

James nodded, his gaze drifting to the street outside where the shadows seemed to dance and shift with a life of their own. "It's like the town is holding its breath, waiting for something."

Their conversation was interrupted by the arrival of the waitress, who placed their orders on the table with a nod. James took a bite of the pie, savoring the sweet and tangy flavor, while Nikki wrapped her hands around her coffee mug, absorbing its warmth.

As they ate, their attention was drawn to a group of locals gathered near the entrance. The conversation was too low to make out, but the tension was palpable. Every so often, one of them would glance towards James and Nikki, their expressions a mix of curiosity and something else—wary, perhaps even suspicious.

Feeling the weight of their stares, James attempted a friendly smile, but the group quickly turned away, resuming their hushed conversation. He exchanged a glance with Nikki, who shrugged slightly, her expression thoughtful.

After finishing their meal, James and Nikki decided to take a walk around the town before night fully descended. The air outside was cooler now, the sky a deep indigo speckled with the first stars of the evening. The streetlights flickered to life as they strolled down the main street, casting a soft, golden glow that barely reached the shadows lurking at the edges.

As they walked, they couldn't shake the feeling of being watched. James glanced over his shoulder more than once, half-expecting to catch sight of someone following them, but the street remained empty save for the occasional cat darting across their path.

They paused at the old fountain, its stone surface weathered by time and the elements. Nikki ran her fingers along the edge, feeling the grooves and indentations that told a story of erosion and neglect. "I wonder how long it's been since this thing last flowed," she mused aloud.

James joined her, peering into the dry basin. "A long time, I'd wager. Like the town itself, it seems to have fallen into a sort of... suspended animation."

Their conversation was interrupted by the eerie sound of the wind sweeping through the narrow alleys, whispering secrets that eluded understanding. As they continued their exploration, they noticed more signs of the town's enigmatic past: weathered plaques with faded inscriptions, murals depicting scenes of a vibrant community long ago, and, most hauntingly, a collection of statues in a small park, their faces worn smooth by time.

The statues depicted figures from history—a soldier, a farmer, a mother and child—but there was something unsettling about them, as if they were more than mere stone. James felt a chill creep up his spine as he studied them, half-expecting the eyes to flick open and fix him with an accusatory stare.

Nikki, sensing his discomfort, took his hand, offering a reassuring squeeze. "We'll uncover the stories here, James. We've done it before."

He nodded, grateful for her presence. Together, they left the park, their footsteps echoing in the stillness. As they made their way back to the car, the streetlights flickered ominously, casting long shadows that seemed to stretch towards them, reaching like ghostly fingers.

The drive to their accommodation—a quaint bed and breakfast on the outskirts of town—was uneventful, though the sense of unease lingered. The B&B, a large Victorian house, welcomed them with its warm glow and the inviting scent of lavender wafting through the air.

Their host, a kindly woman named Mrs. Fletcher, greeted them at the door. Her eyes, sharp and inquisitive, seemed to assess them in a heartbeat. "Welcome to Ravenswood," she said with a smile that didn't quite reach her eyes. "I trust your journey was pleasant?"

"It was, thank you," Nikki replied, returning the smile. "The town is lovely."

Mrs. Fletcher nodded, leading them inside. "It has its charms, though it's not without its mysteries, as you'll likely discover during your stay."

James and Nikki exchanged a knowing glance, intrigued by the hint of something unspoken in her words. After showing them to their room, Mrs. Fletcher bid them goodnight, leaving them to settle in.

The room was cozy, adorned with vintage furniture and soft, floral patterns that spoke of a bygone era. As James and Nikki unpacked, the events of the day played through their minds, each detail adding to the tapestry of their unfolding adventure.

As night enveloped Ravenswood, they sat by the window, watching the town below as it succumbed to the darkness. The streetlights cast an eerie glow, and the wind continued its relentless whispering, as if trying to communicate something important.

"Tomorrow, we'll start digging deeper," Nikki said, her voice confident yet tinged with anticipation.

James nodded, feeling both excitement and trepidation. "Yes, there's much to uncover here. I just hope we're ready for whatever we find."

With that, they turned in for the night, the shadows of Ravenswood keeping silent watch as the town slumbered, holding its secrets close, waiting for the right moment to reveal its true nature.

Chapter 2

Whispers of the Past

The morning sun filtered through the curtains of the cozy Victorian bed and breakfast, casting gentle patterns on the floor. James and Nikki awoke to the sound of distant birdsong and the aroma of freshly brewed coffee wafting from the kitchen below. They exchanged a look of determination; today was the day they would start uncovering the secrets of Ravenswood.

After a hearty breakfast prepared by Mrs. Fletcher, who had softened in demeanor since their arrival, they set off towards the town's library. The streets of Ravenswood were quiet, the morning air crisp and filled with the scent of dew on grass. The library, a modest brick building with ivy creeping up its walls, stood at the end of the main street. Its façade suggested both age and a certain resilience, much like the town itself.

Inside, the library was a sanctuary of hushed whispers and the faint rustling of pages. The scent of old books enveloped them as they stepped through the doors, a comforting reminder of countless stories waiting to be discovered. Behind the main desk sat Mrs. Harris, the town librarian, who looked up from her task with an air of mild disinterest.

"Morning," she greeted, her voice as muted as the library's atmosphere. Her eyes, however, held a spark of curiosity as they assessed the newcomers.

"Good morning," Nikki replied with a warm smile. "We're looking for information about the town's history, particularly around the time of the race riot."

At the mention of the riot, Mrs. Harris's expression shifted, a flicker of something unreadable crossing her face. "That's quite a topic," she said slowly. "Most folks around here prefer to let the past be."

James stepped forward. "We're hoping to learn more about it, maybe find some records or articles from that time."

Mrs. Harris hesitated, her fingers tracing the edge of the desk. "Well, there are some old newspaper clippings and photographs in the archives. They're not often looked at, mind you."

"We'd appreciate any help you can offer," Nikki said, her tone gentle but firm.

With a resigned nod, Mrs. Harris motioned for them to follow her. She led them to a back room where the air was thick with dust and the weight of history. Shelves lined the walls, crammed with boxes labeled with faded handwriting. The librarian gestured to a corner table. "You can use this space. I'll bring you some of the files we have."

As Mrs. Harris disappeared into the labyrinth of archives, James and Nikki settled in, the anticipation of discovery thrumming between them. Moments later, the librarian returned with a stack of yellowed newspapers and a box of photographs.

"These should get you started," she said, placing the materials on the table. "If you need anything else, just holler."

"Thank you," Nikki responded, her gratitude sincere. As Mrs. Harris returned to her desk, James and Nikki began sifting through the remnants of the past.

The newspapers were fragile, their pages brittle from age. Headlines from decades ago spoke of everyday events—the opening of a new store, a local bake sale—and, inevitably, the riot. The articles were brief, sparse on details, almost as if the writers were reluctant to commit the events to print. Yet, the language hinted at the chaos and violence that had once erupted in the town.

Nikki's fingers traced the faded ink, her mind piecing together fragments of a larger narrative. "Look at this," she murmured, pointing to a paragraph describing the aftermath of the riot. "It mentions a meeting at the town hall that turned violent, but there's no follow-up."

James leaned closer, studying the article. "It's like they wanted to forget it ever happened."

Their attention turned to the photographs next, some sepia-toned, others black and white. They depicted scenes of everyday life in Ravenswood—parades, town gatherings, families posing stiffly in their Sunday best. But there were also images that seemed to pulse with a deeper story. A photograph of the town square, taken after the riot, showed buildings with shattered windows and streets littered with debris. The faces of the townspeople in the photographs were solemn, their expressions haunted.

As they examined the pictures, a strange sensation washed over them. The images seemed to shift subtly when they weren't looking directly at them, as if the photographs were alive, eager to tell their story. James rubbed his eyes, dismissing it as a trick of the light, but the feeling persisted.

Nikki picked up a particularly striking photograph of a group of townspeople gathered in front of a now-dilapidated building. Her eyes lingered on the faces, trying to discern their emotions. "It's like they're looking right through us," she said softly.

James nodded in agreement, a shiver skimming his spine. "Do you think these people are still around? Their descendants, maybe?"

"Possibly," Nikki replied, setting the photo aside. "But convincing them to talk about what happened might be a challenge."

Their examination was interrupted by the sound of footsteps. Mrs. Harris appeared, her expression somewhat softer than before. "How are you two getting along?"

"We've found some interesting articles and photos," James replied. "But there's still so much we don't understand."

Mrs. Harris hesitated, then sighed. "The riot was a dark time for Ravenswood. Many people were hurt, and the town has tried to move on without looking back. But some things… they don't stay buried."

Nikki sensed an opportunity and pressed gently. "Is there anyone who might be willing to talk to us, someone who remembers or knows the stories?"

The librarian considered their request, her gaze distant. "There's a few old-timers who might have something to say, but they're not easy to get to talk. Mr. Johnson, at the hardware store, was around back then. He might know more than he lets on."

"Thank you, Mrs. Harris," Nikki said, her gratitude genuine. "We appreciate any leads you can give us."

Mrs. Harris nodded, a ghost of a smile on her lips. "Just be careful. Not everyone likes outsiders poking into old wounds."

With the librarian's words echoing in their minds, James and Nikki continued to pore over the materials, piecing together the fragments of Ravenswood's past. As the hours slipped by, they were drawn deeper into a tapestry of intrigue, secrets, and shadows—an intricate web that seemed determined to pull them in.

Outside, the day grew warmer, casting long shadows across the town. As their research unfolded, the couple found themselves not only uncovering the town's history but also becoming a part of it. Each discovery brought them closer to understanding the events that had shaped Ravenswood and the ghosts that lingered, waiting for their stories to be told.

As they prepared to leave the library, Mrs. Harris approached them once more, her demeanor a touch more open. "If you need more time with the archives, just let me know. I'll see what else I can dig up for you."

James and Nikki exchanged a grateful glance. "We'll definitely take you up on that," James said. "And thank you again for your help."

Mrs. Harris nodded, a hint of warmth in her eyes. "Just remember, not all stories have happy endings."

Leaving the library, they stepped into the afternoon sunlight, feeling both the weight of their discoveries and the promise of more to come. As they walked back towards the town center, the echo of Mrs. Harris's words lingered—a reminder of the complexity of history and the courage required to face it.

Their next stop was the hardware store, where they hoped to find Mr. Johnson and perhaps gain a deeper insight into the events that had left such a profound mark on Ravenswood. The store, a quaint establishment with a wide porch and a sign that creaked in the breeze, seemed to embody the essence of small-town America.

Inside, the scent of sawdust and metal filled the air, mingling with the warmth of the afternoon. Mr. Johnson, a silver-haired gentleman with a sturdy frame, was organizing shelves when they entered. His eyes, sharp and inquisitive, met theirs with a mix of curiosity and caution.

"Afternoon," he greeted, his voice carrying the weight of years and experiences. "Looking for something specific?"

James introduced himself and Nikki, explaining their interest in the town's history and the riot. Mr. Johnson's expression shifted slightly, a flicker of something passing through his eyes—an acknowledgment of a shared past, perhaps.

"That was a long time ago," he said, his tone measured. "Most folks around here have moved on, but the memories… they linger."

Nikki stepped forward, her voice gentle. "We're trying to understand what happened, to piece together the story from those who were there."

Mr. Johnson regarded them for a moment, as if weighing their sincerity. Finally, he nodded, a hint of resignation in his posture. "Alright. I'll tell you what I remember, but it won't be easy to hear."

He led them to a small sitting area at the back of the store, offering them seats. As they settled in, he began to speak, his voice steady but tinged with the weight of remembrance.

"The riot... it started with a meeting gone wrong. Tensions were high, and folks were on edge. Words were exchanged, and before anyone knew it, things turned violent. People were hurt, lives were lost. It was chaos."

James listened intently, his mind capturing every detail. "Why did it happen? What sparked it?"

Mr. Johnson sighed, his gaze distant. "Fear, mostly. Fear and ignorance. People were scared of change, of what they didn't understand. It's a story as old as time."

Nikki met his eyes, understanding the depth of his words. "And the town... how did it cope afterward?"

"Some tried to forget, others left. But the scars remained," Mr. Johnson replied, his voice tinged with regret. "It's like a wound that never truly heals."

Silence settled over them, the weight of history palpable in the air. James and Nikki exchanged a glance, each sensing the enormity of the truth they were uncovering.

"Thank you for sharing this with us," Nikki said, her gratitude sincere. "We hope to honor the stories of those who lived through it."

Mr. Johnson nodded, a flicker of warmth in his eyes. "Just remember, the past is a part of us, but it doesn't have to define us. We have the power to shape what comes next."

As they left the hardware store, the sun began its descent, casting a golden glow over Ravenswood. The day had offered them a glimpse into the town's soul, a tapestry woven with threads of pain and resilience.

Walking through the streets, James and Nikki felt the weight of their discoveries, the whisper of the past echoing around them. They knew their journey was far from over, that more secrets were waiting to be unearthed. But with each step, they grew more determined, more committed to uncovering the truth and giving voice to those who had been silenced.

As they returned to the bed and breakfast, the sun dipped below the horizon, leaving behind a sky painted in hues of amber and violet. The town settled into the quiet embrace of evening, the shadows lengthening, the whispers of history growing louder.

As night enveloped Ravenswood, James and Nikki prepared for the challenges ahead. They knew the path they had chosen was fraught with uncertainty and danger, but they were undeterred. Together, they would face the echoes of the past, shining a light on the darkness and seeking justice for those whose stories had not been told.

Chapter 3

Night Terrors

As the night deepened over Ravenswood, the town was shrouded in a silent, eerie stillness. The wind whispered secrets through the branches of ancient trees, and the stars were obscured by a veil of clouds, casting the streets into a deep, unsettling darkness.

In the quaint bed and breakfast on the outskirts of town, James and Nikki lay in their bed, the events of the day swirling in their minds. The room, usually a haven of comfort, felt different that night—charged with a peculiar energy that set their nerves on edge. The floral wallpaper seemed to ripple in the dim light, and the antique furniture cast distorted shadows against the walls.

Nikki tossed and turned, her thoughts a tangled web of curiosity and unease. Each time she closed her eyes, the faces from the photographs they had examined at the library haunted her—solemn, accusing, as if demanding answers. She couldn't shake the feeling that they had disturbed something ancient, something that had lain dormant for too long.

Beside her, James lay awake, his eyes fixed on the ceiling. He too felt the weight of the town's past pressing down on him, a palpable presence that refused to be ignored. The air was thick with anticipation, as if the very walls were holding their breath, waiting for a revelation.

Eventually, exhaustion claimed them both, and they drifted into a restless sleep. But the reprieve was short-lived.

Nikki found herself standing in the town square, yet it was not the quiet, neglected place they had explored earlier. Instead, it was alive with a ghostly resonance of the past. The square was teeming with people, their faces indistinct yet charged with emotion—anger, fear, desperation. The air crackled with tension, and the sky above was a swirling canvas of stormy grays and blacks.

She watched as the scene unfolded—the crowd surging forward, voices raised in a cacophony of protest and panic. The sound of shattering glass and distant screams echoed through the air, mingling with the acrid scent of smoke. It felt so real, so immediate, that she could almost taste the fear and despair.

In the midst of the chaos, Nikki caught sight of a figure standing apart from the crowd, their face obscured by shadow. The figure seemed to be watching her, their gaze penetrating through the tumult. A shiver ran down her spine as she felt an inexplicable connection to this apparition, as if they were trying to convey a message just beyond the reach of her understanding.

Suddenly, the figure raised an arm, pointing towards something behind her. Nikki turned, her heart racing, and found herself staring at the dry fountain in the center of the square. But it wasn't dry anymore—water bubbled up from its depths, tinged with an eerie red hue. The sight filled her with a sense of impending dread, and she knew instinctively that this was not just a dream.

Meanwhile, in his own restless slumber, James was grappling with his own visions. He found himself walking through the woods on the outskirts of town, the moon casting long, sinister shadows that danced along the ground. The air was heavy with silence, broken only by the distant rustle of leaves.

As he moved deeper into the forest, he felt an unseen presence watching him, following his every step. The sensation was unnerving, like a thousand eyes fixed upon him, yet he saw no one. The trees loomed overhead, their branches twisting like skeletal fingers reaching out to ensnare him.

In the distance, he heard a faint whispering, voices calling his name with an urgency that sent chills skittering across his skin. He tried to make out the words, but they eluded him, slipping away like smoke through his fingers. The voices grew louder, more insistent, as if pleading for him to listen, to understand.

Suddenly, the ground beneath him shifted, and he stumbled, falling to his knees. As he looked up, he saw them—figures emerging from the shadows, their faces obscured by darkness. They surrounded him, their presence oppressive and suffocating. He could feel their anger, their pain, radiating outward, enveloping him in a shroud of despair.

One of the figures stepped forward, extending a hand towards him. In their palm lay a small, tarnished locket, its surface engraved with intricate patterns. James reached out to take it, his fingers brushing against the cold metal. As he did, a jolt of understanding coursed through him, and he was filled with a sense of urgency, a need to act.

James awoke with a start, his heart pounding in his chest, the remnants of the dream clinging to him like a dense fog. He sat up, drawing in deep, ragged breaths as he tried to shake off the lingering fear. The room was dark, save for the faint glow of moonlight filtering through the curtains, casting pale shadows across the bed.

Beside him, Nikki stirred, her own sleep disrupted by the intensity of her vision. She blinked, disoriented, the images from her dream still vivid in her mind. The unease that had settled over her earlier had intensified, coiling around her like a living thing.

"Did you dream too?" James asked, his voice hushed, as if speaking too loudly might summon the specters of their nightmares.

Nikki nodded, her expression troubled. "It was like being there, in the middle of it all. The riot... the chaos. It felt so real."

James ran a hand through his hair, trying to make sense of it all. "I was in the woods. There were... people, spirits, maybe. They were trying to tell me something. I could feel their anger."

They sat in silence for a moment, the weight of their shared experience heavy between them. It was as if the town itself had reached out to them, pulling them into its dark history, demanding that they bear witness to the pain that had been buried for so long.

"Do you think it means something?" Nikki asked, her voice tinged with uncertainty. "Are we... are we in danger?"

James hesitated, considering the implications of their dreams. "I don't know. But it feels like we've stirred something up, something that doesn't want to be ignored."

Nikki shivered, drawing the blankets tighter around her. "The town is haunted, James. Not just by ghosts, but by the weight of what happened here."

He reached for her hand, offering what comfort he could. "We'll figure it out. We have to. For the people who lived through it, and for ourselves."

They lay back down, the darkness pressing in around them like a living entity. Sleep came fitfully, haunted by fragments of dreams and whispered voices that refused to be silenced.

The next morning dawned gray and overcast, the air thick with a sense of foreboding. As James and Nikki prepared for the day, the memories of their dreams lingered, casting a shadow over their thoughts.

Their first stop was the library, where they hoped to continue their research and perhaps find some answers to the questions that plagued them. Mrs. Harris greeted them with a nod, her expression more open than the day before.

"Back for more digging?" she asked, her voice carrying a hint of amusement.

James managed a smile, though it felt strained. "Yes, there's still so much we don't know."

Mrs. Harris nodded, gesturing towards the archives. "Help yourselves. I found a few more boxes that might be of interest."

As they settled into their work, the atmosphere in the library was hushed, the weight of history palpable in the air. They sifted through more old newspapers, photographs, and journals, piecing together the fragments of Ravenswood's past.

But the longer they worked, the more Nikki felt a prickling sensation at the back of her neck, as if they were being watched. She glanced around, but the library was empty save for Mrs. Harris, absorbed in her own tasks.

The feeling persisted, a creeping unease that gnawed at the edges of her concentration. She leaned closer to James, her voice a whisper. "Do you feel that? Like we're not alone?"

James paused, considering her words. "Yeah, I've felt it too. Ever since last night... it's like the town is alive, watching us."

They continued their research, but the sense of being observed never left them, a constant presence that added to the growing tension.

Later, as they left the library and made their way through the town, the sensation intensified. The streets were quiet, the usual bustle of daily life muted. The townspeople they passed seemed distant, their faces drawn, as if burdened by some unseen weight.

James and Nikki walked in silence, their thoughts consumed by the events of the previous night. The line between reality and nightmare had blurred, leaving them questioning what was real and what was imagined.

As they approached the town square, Nikki's gaze was drawn to the fountain, its stone surface weathered and cracked. In the daylight, it seemed innocuous, a relic of a bygone era. But in her mind's eye, she saw it as it had appeared in her dream—alive with an unnatural, crimson glow.

She shuddered, turning away from the unsettling vision. "We need to find out more," she said, her voice firm with determination. "About the riot, the people, everything."

James nodded, sharing her resolve. "We should talk to Mr. Johnson again. He might know more than he let on."

With a renewed sense of purpose, they headed towards the hardware store, their minds set on uncovering the truth. The town's secrets were a tangled web, and they were determined to unravel it, no matter the cost.

Inside the hardware store, Mr. Johnson was busy sorting through stock, his demeanor as unassuming as ever. He looked up as they entered, a flicker of recognition in his eyes.

"Back again?" he asked, his voice carrying a note of curiosity.

James approached him, his expression earnest. "We need to know more, about the riot and what happened afterward. Can you help us?"

Mr. Johnson hesitated, a shadow passing over his face. "You're digging into things best left alone," he warned, though his tone was more resigned than admonitory.

Nikki stepped forward, her voice gentle but insistent. "We've had dreams, visions, of the riot. It feels like the town is trying to tell us something."

The older man regarded them for a moment, as if weighing their sincerity. Finally, he sighed, setting aside his work. "Alright, come with me."

He led them to a back room, cluttered with tools and boxes. From a shelf, he retrieved a dusty old ledger, its pages yellowed with age. "This belonged to my father," he explained, opening it to reveal a collection of handwritten notes and entries. "He kept a record of everything that happened back then."

James and Nikki leaned in, their eyes scanning the pages. The entries detailed the events leading up to the riot, the rising tensions, the fears and prejudices that had fueled the violence.

Mr. Johnson pointed to a particular entry, his finger tracing the lines. "This was the night of the meeting that sparked it all. Things got out of hand fast, and once it started, there was no stopping it."

Nikki's heart ached at the words, the raw emotion captured in the faded ink. "Why didn't anyone stop it? Why let it happen?"

Mr. Johnson's expression was somber, his gaze distant. "People were scared, caught up in the frenzy. It's easy to lose sight of what's right when fear takes hold."

James felt a knot of anger and sadness tighten in his chest. "And afterward? How did the town cope?"

"Some tried to forget, others left. But the scars remained," Mr. Johnson replied, echoing the words he had spoken before. "It's a wound that never truly heals."

They spent the next hour poring over the ledger, the weight of the past heavy in the air. The details were stark and sobering, painting a picture of a community torn apart by violence and mistrust.

As they prepared to leave, Mr. Johnson offered them a piece of advice. "Be careful. Not everyone will want you uncovering these old wounds."

"Thank you," James said, his gratitude genuine. "We'll be careful."

As they stepped back into the street, the afternoon sun had begun its descent, casting long shadows across the town. The weight of their discoveries hung heavy on their shoulders, a reminder of the darkness that lay at the heart of Ravenswood.

That night, as they settled in at the bed and breakfast, the unease that had plagued them resurfaced, stronger than ever. The room felt colder, the walls closing in around them with an oppressive weight.

James and Nikki exchanged a glance, their shared resolve firm in the face of mounting fear. They knew the path they had chosen was fraught with danger, but they were determined to see it through.

As they drifted into an uneasy sleep, the whispers returned, threading through their dreams with a haunting persistence. The line between reality and nightmare blurred once more, drawing them deeper into the town's dark history, demanding that they listen, that they understand.

And so, the night wore on, filled with ghostly apparitions and echoes of the past, each revelation bringing them closer to the truth and the justice that had eluded the town for so long.

Chapter 4

Unearthed Secrets

The morning light filtered through the narrow window of the bed and breakfast, casting a soft glow across the room. James and Nikki sat at the small wooden table, their breakfast untouched, as they reviewed their notes from the previous day. The weight of their dreams still clung to them, a reminder of the town's haunting history that refused to be forgotten.

"We need to dig deeper," Nikki said, her voice firm despite the unease that lingered. "There has to be more to the story than what we've uncovered so far."

James nodded, his determination matching hers. "I agree. Mr. Johnson's ledger was a start, but it feels like there are pieces missing. Something bigger is at play here, something that's been hidden for too long."

With a shared resolve, they decided to visit the abandoned building at the edge of town, a place that had been mentioned in Mr. Johnson's ledger. The building, once a bustling community center, had been left to decay after the riot. Rumors whispered that it held secrets buried within its walls—secrets that might finally shed light on the events that had torn Ravenswood apart.

The path to the building was overgrown with weeds, the pavement cracked and uneven beneath their feet. As they approached, the structure loomed ominously against the gray sky, its windows shattered and its doors hanging ajar. Despite its dilapidated state, there was an undeniable sense of history clinging to it, a silent witness to the past.

James and Nikki paused at the entrance, exchanging a glance filled with both anticipation and trepidation. Taking a deep breath, they stepped inside, the floorboards creaking ominously beneath their weight. Dust motes danced in the air, caught in the shafts of light that pierced through the broken windows.

The interior was a ghostly echo of its former self. Faded posters clung to the walls, their messages long forgotten. A few broken chairs lay scattered across the floor, remnants of the meetings and gatherings that had once filled the space. The air was thick with the scent of mildew and decay, yet beneath it lingered the faint, haunting aroma of old wood and memories.

As they explored the building, they were drawn to a particular corner, where the floorboards seemed to resonate with a peculiar energy. Nikki knelt down, brushing away the dust to reveal a trapdoor hidden beneath the grime. Her heart quickened at the discovery, and she gestured for James to join her.

"Do you think this is it?" she asked, her voice barely above a whisper.

James nodded, his excitement tempered by caution. "It has to be. Let's see what's down there."

With careful fingers, they pried the trapdoor open, revealing a narrow staircase descending into darkness. The air that wafted up was cool and musty, carrying with it the promise of secrets long buried. Armed with flashlights, they descended the stairs, each step taking them deeper into the heart of the building and its hidden mysteries.

At the bottom of the stairs, they found themselves in a small, dimly lit room. The walls were lined with shelves, each one crammed with boxes, old files, and relics of the past. A single, dust-covered table stood at the center, its surface littered with yellowed papers and faded photographs.

Nikki's eyes widened as she took in the sight, the magnitude of their discovery settling over her. "This must be it," she murmured, reaching for one of the boxes. "The records of what really happened."

James joined her, his hands trembling slightly as he lifted the lid of another box. Inside, he found folders filled with documents, their edges frayed with age. As he sifted through them, he realized they were records of meetings, correspondence, and police reports—evidence of a story that had been deliberately concealed.

"This is incredible," James said, his voice tinged with awe. "It's like a hidden archive of the town's history."

Nikki nodded, her attention drawn to a collection of photographs scattered across the table. She picked up one of the images, her heart aching at the sight. It depicted the town square in the aftermath of the riot, the buildings damaged and the streets strewn with debris. The faces of the townspeople were solemn, their expressions haunted by the events they had witnessed.

As they continued to explore the room, they uncovered more documents—letters from town officials, reports of meetings that had taken place behind closed doors, and accounts of the escalating tensions that had eventually led to violence. The picture they painted was one of betrayal, fear, and a desperate attempt to maintain control.

Armed with this new evidence, James and Nikki knew they needed to confront Mr. Johnson once more. The ledger he had shared with them had been only a small part of the truth, and they needed to understand the full scope of what had happened.

They returned to the hardware store, their minds racing with questions. Mr. Johnson was busy at the counter when they arrived, his demeanor as stoic as ever. He looked up as they entered, his eyes narrowing slightly at the sight of their determined expressions.

"We found something," James said without preamble, placing a stack of documents on the counter. "In the abandoned building."

Mr. Johnson's expression shifted, a flicker of something crossing his face—guilt, perhaps, or resignation. "I see," he replied, his voice measured. "I suppose it was only a matter of time before someone found it."

Nikki stepped forward, her gaze steady. "Why didn't you tell us about this? About the cover-up?"

The older man sighed, his shoulders slumping slightly. "Because it's a part of the town's history that most folks would rather forget. It's easier to bury the past than to face it."

"But that doesn't make it right," James argued, the frustration evident in his voice. "People deserve to know the truth."

Mr. Johnson met their eyes, his expression weary. "You're right. And maybe it's time for the truth to come out. But you have to understand, back then, people were scared. The riot... it shook the town to its core. The powers that be did what they thought was necessary to keep the peace."

Nikki's heart ached at the admission, the weight of untold truths pressing down on her. "And what about the victims? The people who suffered because of it? They deserve justice."

Mr. Johnson nodded, a somber understanding in his gaze. "Yes, they do. And maybe you can help give them that. But be careful. Not everyone will welcome the truth with open arms."

As they left the hardware store, James and Nikki felt the enormity of their task looming before them. The town's history was a tangled web of secrets and lies, and unraveling it would require more than just determination—it would require allies.

Their first stop was the library, where Mrs. Harris greeted them with a nod. Her demeanor was more open than it had been during their initial visits, as if she sensed the shift in their purpose.

"You've found something, haven't you?" she asked, her voice carrying a hint of curiosity.

James nodded, setting the stack of documents on the table. "We found records in the abandoned building. Evidence of a cover-up."

Mrs. Harris's eyes widened, a flicker of surprise crossing her face. "I knew there was more to the story, but I didn't realize the extent of it."

Nikki leaned forward, her expression earnest. "We need your help, Mrs. Harris. We need to gather as much information as we can and find others who might be willing to support us."

The librarian considered their request, her gaze distant. "I can reach out to some of the older residents, those who remember what happened. There are a few who might be willing to talk, if approached the right way."

James and Nikki exchanged a grateful glance, the sense of solidarity bolstering their resolve. "Thank you," Nikki said, her gratitude sincere. "We'll need all the help we can get."

As the day wore on, they continued their quest for allies, reaching out to various residents and sharing the evidence they had uncovered. The reactions were mixed—some were intrigued, others skeptical, and a few outright hostile. But amidst the resistance, they found a small but growing group of supporters, individuals who believed in the importance of truth and justice.

One of their most unexpected allies was Maya, a young activist who had recently moved to Ravenswood. Her passion for social justice and her determination to make a difference made her an invaluable asset to their cause.

"I've heard whispers about the riot since I got here," Maya admitted when they met at a local café. "But no one's been willing to talk about it openly. If you're trying to bring the truth to light, count me in."

With Maya's help, they began to organize a meeting, a chance for the townspeople to come together and discuss the events of the past. It was a risky move, one that could either unite the community or drive it further apart. But they knew it was a necessary step in their journey towards healing and reconciliation.

As they returned to the hidden room in the abandoned building, James and Nikki felt a renewed sense of purpose. The documents they had found were more than just records—they were a testament to the courage and resilience of those who had lived through the riot, a reminder that the past could not be silenced forever.

They spent hours sifting through the files, piecing together the narrative of betrayal and cover-up that had shaped Ravenswood's history. Each document, each photograph, was a thread in a tapestry of pain and perseverance, a story that demanded to be told.

Among the papers, they discovered a series of letters exchanged between town officials and outside parties, evidence of a concerted effort to suppress the truth and maintain the status quo. The implications were staggering, and they knew they had to proceed carefully, aware of the potential consequences of their actions.

As they worked, they were struck by the resilience of the people whose stories they were uncovering. Despite the attempts to erase their experiences, their voices remained, a powerful reminder of the strength of the human spirit.

With their newfound allies and the evidence they had gathered, James and Nikki began to formulate a plan. They would present their findings at the community meeting, offering the townspeople a chance to confront the past and decide how to move forward.

It was a daunting task, but they were determined to see it through. The ghosts of Ravenswood demanded justice, and they were resolved to answer that call, no matter the cost.

As they prepared for the meeting, they felt a sense of anticipation and trepidation. The truth, once revealed, could not be ignored, and they knew they were on the brink of a pivotal moment in the town's history.

As evening descended over Ravenswood, James and Nikki returned to the bed and breakfast, their minds racing with the possibilities of what lay ahead. The room was quiet, the shadows lengthening as the sun dipped below the horizon.

They sat together, reviewing their notes and discussing their strategy for the meeting. It was a moment of calm before the storm, a chance to gather their thoughts and prepare for the challenges that awaited them.

"We're doing the right thing," Nikki said, her voice filled with conviction. "This is our chance to make a difference, to help the town heal."

James nodded, his resolve unwavering. "I know. And whatever happens, we'll face it together."

As they settled in for the night, the whispers of the past seemed to fade, replaced by a sense of purpose and hope. The road ahead was uncertain, but they were ready to meet it head-on, driven by a shared commitment to uncovering the truth and honoring the memories of those who had come before.

Chapter 5

Shadows in the Daylight

As the morning sun rose over Ravenswood, casting its golden glow across the small town, James and Nikki found themselves enveloped in an uneasy calm. The events of the previous day—the revelations in the hidden room and their confrontation with Mr. Johnson—had left them both exhausted and determined. The truth was slowly unraveling, but with each discovery came a growing sense of dread.

The day began with the familiar routine of breakfast at the bed and breakfast. Yet, even in the comfort of their temporary home, James and Nikki couldn't shake the feeling that they were not alone. As they sipped their coffee, eyes seemed to follow them from the shadows, an unseen presence lurking just beyond their perception.

Nikki glanced out the window, her gaze scanning the street below. "Do you feel it?" she asked, her voice barely above a whisper.

James nodded, his own eyes darting to the corners of the room. "It's like someone's watching us. Ever since we found those documents, I can't shake the feeling that we're being followed."

Their conversation was interrupted by the arrival of Mrs. Fletcher, their hospitable yet enigmatic host. Her smile was warm, but there was an undercurrent of something else—concern, perhaps.

"Everything alright?" Mrs. Fletcher inquired, her eyes flickering with curiosity.

Nikki forced a smile, unwilling to burden their host with their growing paranoia. "Yes, just a bit tired from all the research."

The older woman nodded, though her expression remained thoughtful. "Well, if you need anything, don't hesitate to ask."

As Mrs. Fletcher departed, James and Nikki exchanged a look, their unspoken fears echoing between them. They knew they needed to remain vigilant, to trust their instincts even as they delved deeper into the mysteries surrounding Ravenswood.

Determined to continue their investigation, James and Nikki set out for the day, their destination the town square. The streets of Ravenswood, usually bustling with the sounds of daily life, were eerily quiet, the only noise the distant chirping of birds and the rustle of leaves in the light breeze.

As they walked, the sensation of being watched persisted, an invisible weight pressing down on them. Every so often, they would catch sight of movement out of the corner of their eyes—a flicker of shadow that vanished the moment they turned to look. It was as if the town itself was alive, its very essence observing them with a silent, inscrutable gaze.

Their first stop was the general store, where they hoped to gather more supplies for their research. Inside, the atmosphere was subdued, the patrons going about their business with a quiet efficiency. Yet, James couldn't shake the feeling that they were being scrutinized, that every whisper and glance was directed at them.

Nikki, sensing his discomfort, leaned closer. "We need to be careful. I think people are starting to notice us."

James nodded, his expression grim. "I know. Let's just get what we need and get out of here."

As they made their way through the aisles, Nikki's attention was drawn to a display near the back of the store. There, amidst the shelves of canned goods and household items, stood a rack of local newspapers. The headline of the most recent edition caught her eye: "Outsiders Stirring Up Old Wounds."

Her heart skipped a beat as she scanned the article, the words confirming her suspicions. The townspeople were growing wary, their mistrust fueled by whispers and speculation. It was a dangerous situation, one that could easily spiral out of control if they weren't careful.

"We need to keep our heads down," Nikki murmured, showing James the article. "We can't afford to draw any more attention to ourselves."

James agreed, a knot of anxiety tightening in his chest. They completed their purchases quickly, avoiding eye contact with the other shoppers, and made their way back into the street.

As they walked towards the library, their minds weighed down by the implications of the article, they were stopped by a voice calling out from a nearby alleyway.

"Hey, you two!"

James and Nikki turned to see a man standing in the shadows, his features obscured by the brim of a worn hat. His posture was tense, as if caught between the urge to approach and the instinct to flee.

"Can we help you?" James asked, his voice cautious.

The man hesitated, glancing around as if wary of being overheard. "You don't know what you're getting into," he said, his voice low and urgent. "This town... it's not what it seems. You need to leave while you still can."

Nikki's curiosity flared, but she held her ground. "Why? What's happening here?"

The stranger shifted, his gaze restless. "There are things in this town, things that are better left buried. People don't take kindly to outsiders poking around."

James felt a chill skitter down his spine. "Are you threatening us?"

The man shook his head, his expression earnest. "No, it's a warning. For your own good. The shadows here... they have a way of swallowing people whole."

Before they could ask more, the stranger turned and disappeared into the alley, leaving James and Nikki standing in the street, the weight of his words hanging heavy in the air.

Determined to press on despite the warning, they continued to the library, where Mrs. Harris awaited them with an air of quiet anticipation. Her demeanor was more reserved than before, as if she too was aware of the growing tension in the town.

"I'm glad to see you're still here," Mrs. Harris said, her voice tinged with relief. "I heard some rumblings, people talking about your investigation."

James nodded, grateful for her support. "We're being careful, but it's hard not to feel the pressure."

The librarian gestured to a stack of new materials she had gathered for them. "I found some more records for you to look through. They might help fill in some of the gaps."

As they settled into their familiar corner of the library, the sensation of being watched intensified, a prickling awareness that set their nerves on edge. The shadows seemed to deepen, pressing in around them with a silent, malignant presence.

Nikki flipped through the documents, her mind racing with the implications of their discoveries. Each piece of information brought them closer to the truth, but also deeper into the web of secrets and lies that had ensnared Ravenswood for so long.

"We're onto something big," Nikki whispered, her voice barely audible. "But we're not the only ones who know it."

James nodded, his focus unwavering. "We have to keep going, no matter what. The truth is too important."

As the day wore on, James and Nikki left the library, their minds buzzing with new insights and a growing sense of urgency. The streets were still, the air heavy with an unnatural silence that seemed to amplify their every step.

Their route took them past the old fountain in the town square, its dry basin a stark reminder of the town's faded glory. As they paused to catch their breath, Nikki's gaze was drawn to the shadows lurking at the edges of the square.

There, half-hidden by the encroaching darkness, stood a figure—a shadowy silhouette that seemed to flicker and shift with the breeze. For a moment, Nikki thought she saw eyes glinting in the gloom, watching them with an intensity that sent a shiver skittering across her skin.

"James," she whispered, her voice tense. "Do you see that?"

James followed her gaze, his breath catching as he too noticed the figure. But before he could speak, the silhouette dissolved into the shadows, leaving behind an unsettling emptiness.

"We need to go," James said, his voice firm.

They hurried away from the square, their footsteps echoing in the stillness. The feeling of being followed persisted, an invisible presence trailing them through the streets, always just out of sight.

As they made their way back to the bed and breakfast, the unease that had haunted them all day began to coalesce into a tangible fear. The town seemed to close in around them, its once-charming streets now fraught with hidden dangers and unseen adversaries.

Mrs. Fletcher greeted them with her usual warmth, but there was a shadow of concern in her eyes. "You two look like you've seen a ghost," she remarked, her tone light but probing.

James forced a smile, unwilling to reveal the full extent of their anxiety. "Just tired," he replied. "It's been a long day."

As they retreated to the privacy of their room, the weight of the day's events settled over them like a shroud. The shadows seemed to stretch and writhe, a living entity that defied explanation.

In the quiet sanctity of their room, James and Nikki sat together, their minds racing with questions and possibilities. The warning from the stranger, the shadows that seemed to pursue them, the growing tension in the town—it all pointed to something larger, something that threatened to engulf them if they weren't careful.

"We're in over our heads," Nikki admitted, her voice tinged with apprehension. "But we can't turn back now."

James nodded, his resolve solidifying. "No, we can't. The truth is out there, and we're the only ones who can bring it to light."

They sat in silence for a moment, the enormity of their task settling over them like a mantle. The shadows danced at the edge of their vision, a constant reminder of the stakes they faced.

"We have to be careful," James said finally, his voice steady. "But we have to keep going. For the people who lived through it, for the town... and for ourselves."

Nikki met his gaze, her expression filled with determination. "Together, then. No matter what."

As they prepared for another restless night, the shadows continued to press in around them, whispering secrets and promises that eluded understanding. But despite the fear, they found strength in their shared purpose, a beacon of light amidst the encroaching darkness.

As night fell over Ravenswood, the town settled into a restless slumber, its secrets and shadows weaving a tapestry of mystery and intrigue. James and Nikki lay awake, their minds attuned to the whispers of the past, the promise of discovery guiding them forward.

The shadows remained, a constant presence that defied explanation, but they had made a pact to face them together. And as the night deepened, they held onto the hope that the truth would ultimately prevail, illuminating the darkness and bringing justice to the forgotten souls who had been silenced for so long.

Together, they would confront the shadows, unravel the mysteries of Ravenswood, and emerge stronger for the trials they faced. For in the heart of darkness lay the promise of light, and they were determined to bring it forth, no matter the cost.

Chapter 6

The Gathering Storm

As the sun dipped below the horizon, casting Ravenswood in a golden hue, James and Nikki prepared for the pivotal community meeting. The room at the local community center was dimly lit, its atmosphere charged with both anticipation and tension. Flyers announcing the meeting had been distributed throughout the town, and whispers about the couple's discoveries had spread like wildfire.

James and Nikki arrived early to set up, their minds abuzz with the weight of what was to come. Tables were arranged in a semicircle, and chairs were positioned to accommodate the expected crowd. A projector was carefully positioned to display the documents and photographs they had uncovered, evidence of the town's troubled past and the cover-up that had kept it hidden.

Maya, the young activist who had become one of their staunchest allies, joined them in their preparations. Her energy was palpable, a beacon of hope amidst the uncertainty. She helped arrange the materials, her determination shining through every action.

"Are you ready for this?" Maya asked, her voice steady despite the gravity of the situation.

Nikki nodded, though her heart fluttered with nerves. "We have to be. This is our chance to bring the truth to light."

James adjusted the projector, his focus intense. "We've done everything we can to prepare. Now it's up to the town to decide what to do with this information."

As the clock ticked closer to the meeting's start time, a few townspeople began to trickle in. Their expressions ranged from curiosity to skepticism, some eyes filled with hope while others carried a shadow of doubt.

Once the room filled and the hum of conversation subsided, Nikki stepped forward to address the gathering. Her voice was clear and confident, carrying the weight of their discoveries and the urgency of their mission.

"Thank you all for coming," she began, meeting the gaze of each attendee. "We're here because we believe Ravenswood deserves to know the truth about its past. We've uncovered documents and evidence that point to a cover-up surrounding the events of the race riot, and we want to share what we've found with all of you."

James took over, his tone earnest and steady. "This isn't just about uncovering the past. It's about understanding our history so we can move forward together. We know this might be difficult to hear, but it's necessary for healing and reconciliation."

The room was silent, the air thick with anticipation. As James and Nikki began to present their findings, the projector cast images of old photographs and documents onto the wall, each one a piece of the puzzle they had worked tirelessly to assemble.

As the presentation unfolded, the reactions of the townspeople varied. Some leaned forward, captivated by the revelations, while others shifted uncomfortably in their seats. Murmurs of disbelief and denial rippled through the crowd, a palpable tension building with each new piece of evidence.

One older gentleman, Mr. Patterson, stood up, a scowl etched on his weathered face. "Why dredge up the past?" he demanded, his voice tinged with anger. "All it's going to do is stir up trouble!"

Nikki met his gaze, her expression calm but resolute. "Because the past is still affecting us today. Ignoring it won't make it go away. We have to confront it if we want to heal and move on."

A woman in the back, Mrs. Jensen, spoke up next, her voice quavering with emotion. "My grandmother was there that day. She always said there were things that didn't add up, that people were too scared to speak the truth."

Maya chimed in, her voice passionate. "This is about justice for those who suffered, for the voices that were silenced. We can't ignore that."

As the discussion continued, the atmosphere in the room began to shift. An inexplicable chill settled over the gathering, the temperature dropping noticeably. The lights flickered, casting eerie shadows that seemed to dance across the walls.

James and Nikki exchanged a glance, their shared unease mirrored in each other's eyes. They had expected resistance, but the sudden change in the room's energy was unsettling.

Without warning, the projector screen flickered, the images distorting before their eyes. The lights dimmed further, and a low, mournful wail echoed through the room, sending a shiver down the spines of those present.

Gasps and murmurs of fear erupted from the crowd, panic spreading like wildfire. Chairs scraped against the floor as people shifted nervously, eyes darting around the room in search of the source of the disturbance.

Nikki stepped forward, her voice a beacon of calm amidst the chaos. "Please, everyone, stay calm. We need to stay together and see this through."

But the room had descended into disarray, fear and superstition taking hold. The shadows seemed to swell, pressing in around them, and the wail grew louder, a haunting lament that tugged at the very fabric of the community.

As the supernatural occurrences continued, the townspeople's fear turned to denial. Some whispered that it was a trick, a ploy to manipulate them. Others were convinced that the spirits of the past were angry, seeking vengeance for the truths that had been buried for so long.

James and Nikki struggled to regain control of the meeting, their voices drowned out by the rising tide of panic. But amidst the chaos, a few voices of reason emerged, urging their fellow townspeople to listen and consider the evidence before them.

Maya, undeterred by the ominous atmosphere, stood firm in her resolve. "This is exactly why we need to confront the past! Ignoring it won't make these things go away. We have to face it, together!"

Her words, though passionate, were nearly lost in the cacophony of fear and disbelief. The meeting, which had started with such promise, seemed on the brink of unraveling entirely.

In the midst of the turmoil, a figure emerged from the shadows at the back of the room. It was Mr. Johnson, the hardware store owner who had been both a source of information and a voice of caution. He stepped forward, his presence commanding attention and quieting the crowd.

"Enough," Mr. Johnson said, his voice steady and authoritative. "This isn't about tricks or vengeance. It's about finding the truth and honoring those who came before us. We owe it to them to listen."

His words cut through the chaos, a moment of clarity amidst the confusion. The room fell silent, the townspeople turning their attention to the man who had lived through the events they were now discussing.

Mr. Johnson met their gaze, his expression one of resolve. "I've seen this town through many changes, and I know we can come through this too. But only if we're willing to face the truth, no matter how uncomfortable it may be."

With Mr. Johnson's intervention, the meeting regained a semblance of order. The supernatural occurrences subsided, leaving behind an uneasy stillness that settled over the room. The townspeople, though still wary, were willing to listen once more.

James and Nikki resumed their presentation, their voices steady and filled with conviction. They spoke of the need for understanding and reconciliation, for acknowledging the past so that Ravenswood could finally heal.

As the meeting drew to a close, the mood in the room had shifted. While fear and resistance still lingered, there was also a sense of possibility—a glimmer of hope that the town might be able to confront its past and forge a new path forward.

Despite the strides made during the meeting, it was clear that Ravenswood remained a town divided. Some left the gathering with renewed determination to uncover the truth, while others clung to their skepticism and fear.

James and Nikki stood at the entrance of the community center as people filed out, their expressions a mix of exhaustion and relief. Maya joined them, her eyes shining with hope.

"We did it," she said, her voice filled with quiet triumph. "We got them to listen."

Nikki nodded, though her thoughts were tinged with uncertainty. "It's a start, but we still have a long way to go."

James placed a hand on her shoulder, offering a reassuring squeeze. "We knew this wouldn't be easy. But we're not alone in this. We have allies, and together, we can make a difference."

As they left the community center, the night air was cool and crisp, a welcome reprieve from the charged atmosphere inside. The streets of Ravenswood were quiet, the town seemingly holding its breath in the aftermath of the meeting.

James, Nikki, and Maya walked together, the weight of the evening's events still fresh in their minds. They knew that the path ahead would be fraught with challenges, but their resolve was stronger than ever.

"We'll keep pushing forward," Maya said, her determination unwavering. "We have to."

Nikki nodded, her heart swelling with gratitude for the allies they had found. "Yes, we will. We've come too far to turn back now."

As they parted ways, James and Nikki made their way back to the bed and breakfast, their minds racing with thoughts of the future. The town's secrets were beginning to unravel, and they were determined to see it through to the end.

That night, as they settled into their room, the shadows seemed less oppressive, the whispers of the past a little quieter. Though the storm of fear and resistance had threatened to overwhelm them, they had weathered it together, emerging stronger and more resolute.

Chapter 7

The Haunting Intensifies

As dawn broke over Ravenswood, the town lay beneath a veil of mist, its streets eerily silent in the early morning light. James and Nikki awoke with a sense of foreboding, the weight of the previous night's meeting heavy on their minds. Though they had made progress in their quest for truth, the atmosphere felt charged with an unspoken tension, as if the very air hummed with anticipation.

The events of the meeting had left the couple with a renewed sense of urgency. The supernatural occurrences had not only unsettled the townspeople but had also served as a stark reminder of the restless spirits that lingered in Ravenswood, demanding justice and recognition for the injustices they had suffered. As James and Nikki prepared to face the day, they knew that the spirits' presence was growing more insistent, their need for resolution becoming impossible to ignore.

As they made their way through the town, the couple could sense the unease that permeated Ravenswood. The townspeople moved with a tentative caution, their eyes scanning the streets as if expecting something unseen to emerge from the shadows. Conversations were hushed, and glances were exchanged with a mixture of fear and curiosity.

James and Nikki stopped by the diner for breakfast, hoping to gauge the mood of the town and perhaps gather any new information. Inside, the usual chatter was subdued, the patrons speaking in low tones as they recounted the events of the previous night. The waitress, who had served them on their first evening in Ravenswood, approached their table with a wary smile.

"Morning," she greeted, her eyes flickering with curiosity. "Quite the meeting last night, huh?"

James nodded, his expression thoughtful. "Yeah, it was something. Did you hear anything about what people are saying?"

The waitress leaned in slightly, her voice dropping to a whisper. "People are spooked, that's for sure. Some think it's a sign, that the spirits are trying to tell us something."

Nikki exchanged a glance with James, her thoughts aligning with the waitress's words. "And what do you think?" she asked, her tone gentle.

The waitress hesitated, then shrugged. "I don't know. But I've lived here long enough to know that this town has its secrets. Maybe it's time for them to come out."

As she moved away to attend to other customers, James and Nikki considered her words. The spirits were indeed trying to communicate, and it was up to them to decipher the message and bring it to light.

Leaving the diner, they decided to visit the library to continue their research. As they walked, the town seemed to hum with an unspoken energy, the air thick with the presence of unseen watchers. James couldn't shake the feeling that they were being followed, though each time he turned to look, he found nothing but empty streets and the occasional stray cat.

Their path took them past the old fountain in the town square, its dry basin a silent witness to the passage of time. As they paused to catch their breath, Nikki's gaze was drawn to a movement out of the corner of her eye—a shadow that flickered and danced at the edge of her vision.

"James, look," she whispered, her voice tinged with urgency.

James followed her gaze, his heart skipping a beat as he saw the same shadowy figure, its form indistinct and ethereal. It hovered near the fountain, its presence palpable yet elusive, as if caught between two worlds.

Before they could react, the shadow dissolved into the mist, leaving behind an unsettling emptiness. James and Nikki exchanged a glance, their shared unease mirrored in each other's eyes.

"We have to keep moving," James said finally, his voice firm with determination.

Nikki nodded, though her heart fluttered with apprehension. "I know. But it's like the spirits are getting stronger, more desperate for us to listen."

Arriving at the library, they were greeted by Mrs. Harris, whose demeanor was more reserved than usual. She gestured for them to follow her to a secluded corner, her expression one of quiet concern.

"I'm glad you're here," Mrs. Harris said, her voice hushed. "Things have been... strange since the meeting. People are talking, and not all of it is friendly."

James nodded, understanding the underlying tension that had gripped the town. "We're trying to help, but it's not easy when people are scared."

Mrs. Harris offered a small, sympathetic smile. "I know. But you're doing important work. I've found some more materials that might help you."

She led them to a table piled high with old newspapers, photographs, and journals, each one a fragment of Ravenswood's haunted past. As they sifted through the documents, the couple felt the weight of history pressing down on them, a reminder of the lives and stories that had been lost to time.

Among the papers, they discovered accounts of other supernatural occurrences, reports of ghostly apparitions and unexplained phenomena that had plagued the town for decades. It was clear that the spirits were not a recent manifestation—they had been present all along, their voices growing louder as the truth sought to break free.

As the day wore on, James and Nikki left the library, their minds racing with the implications of their discoveries. The spirits were becoming more aggressive, their presence more pronounced as they sought justice and recognition for the wrongs they had endured.

The couple decided to visit Mr. Johnson at the hardware store, hoping to gain further insight into the events surrounding the riot and the subsequent cover-up. The store was quiet when they arrived, the usual bustle of customers noticeably absent.

Mr. Johnson greeted them with a nod, his expression thoughtful. "Back for more?" he asked, his voice carrying a hint of curiosity.

Nikki stepped forward, her gaze steady. "We need to know more about the riot, and why the spirits are so restless. Do you have any ideas?"

The older man sighed, his eyes distant as he considered their question. "The riot was a dark time for Ravenswood. People were hurt, and families were torn apart. But the real tragedy is that so many voices were silenced, their stories lost to fear and prejudice."

James listened intently, his mind capturing every detail. "And the spirits? Why are they becoming more active now?"

Mr. Johnson met their gaze, his expression somber. "Because the truth is finally coming to light. They're desperate to be heard, to have their stories told and their suffering acknowledged."

Leaving the hardware store, James and Nikki felt the weight of the spirits' unrest pressing down on them. The town was a tapestry of fear and confusion, its residents caught between the desire for truth and the comfort of denial.

As they made their way back to the bed and breakfast, the shadows seemed to deepen, the air growing colder with each step. The spirits' presence was unmistakable, their whispers threading through the streets like a haunting melody that refused to be silenced.

Inside the bed and breakfast, Mrs. Fletcher greeted them with her usual warmth, though her eyes held a hint of concern. "You two look like you've seen a ghost," she remarked, her tone light but probing.

James managed a wry smile, though his heart was heavy with the burden of their quest. "Something like that. It's been a long day."

As they retreated to the privacy of their room, the weight of the spirits' demands settled over them like a shroud. The shadows seemed to stretch and writhe, a living entity that defied explanation.

That evening, as darkness fell over Ravenswood, the spirits made their presence known in new and unsettling ways. Objects in their room began to move of their own accord—a book sliding off the shelf, a chair creaking as if under an unseen weight. The air was thick with an electric charge, a palpable tension that set their nerves on edge.

Nikki sat on the edge of the bed, her heart racing as she watched the phenomena unfold. "James, do you see that?" she asked, her voice barely above a whisper.

James nodded, his own unease mirrored in her eyes. "I do. It's like they're trying to communicate, to make us understand."

The room was filled with a chorus of ghostly whispers, voices that seemed to echo from the very walls. Though the words were indistinct, the urgency of their message was undeniable—a plea for justice, a demand for recognition.

As the night wore on, James and Nikki knew they needed to take action. The spirits' desperation was growing, their presence more insistent with each passing moment. They had to find a way to bring peace to the restless souls and uncover the full truth of what had happened in Ravenswood.

"We need to figure out what they're trying to tell us," Nikki said, her voice filled with determination. "We can't ignore this any longer."

James nodded, his resolve matching hers. "You're right. We have to keep pushing, no matter what."

They spent the remainder of the night planning their next steps, their minds focused on the task ahead. The spirits were counting on them, and they were determined to honor the voices of the past, to bring justice and healing to a town haunted by its own history.

As dawn broke over Ravenswood once more, James and Nikki felt a renewed sense of purpose. The spirits' presence, though unsettling, was also a reminder of the importance of their mission. They were not alone in their quest for truth—an entire community of souls, both living and departed, was counting on them to bring the past to light.

With each new day, they drew closer to unraveling the mysteries of Ravenswood, to bridging the gap between the present and the past. The journey was fraught with danger and uncertainty, but they were determined to see it through to the end.

Chapter 8

Allies and Adversaries

As the sun rose over Ravenswood, casting a hazy glow over the town, James and Nikki awoke with a renewed sense of determination. The previous night had been fraught with supernatural occurrences and an ever-present sense of unease, but the couple was resolute in their mission to uncover the truth and bring peace to the restless spirits that haunted the town.

Their first task was to gather their allies—those who believed in their cause and were willing to stand with them against the entrenched forces of fear and denial. They had already found an unexpected supporter in Maya, the young activist whose passion and energy had been a beacon amidst the darkness.

Maya had organized a small gathering at her home, inviting a few trusted residents who were open-minded and curious about the couple's discoveries. As James and Nikki arrived, they were greeted with warm smiles and nods of encouragement, a welcome reprieve from the tension that had gripped the town.

Inside, the atmosphere was one of camaraderie and shared purpose. The group sat in a circle, their expressions a mix of curiosity and determination. Maya introduced them one by one: Mrs. Jensen, the woman whose grandmother had witnessed the riot; Mr. Lee, a local historian with a passion for uncovering hidden truths; and Sarah, a schoolteacher who believed in the power of education to change hearts and minds.

"Thank you all for coming," James began, his voice steady despite the weight of their task. "We've uncovered evidence of a cover-up surrounding the events of the race riot, and we believe the spirits of those who suffered are still here, seeking justice."

Nikki took over, her tone earnest. "We can't do this alone. We need your help to bring the truth to light, to honor the memories of those who have been silenced."

Mrs. Jensen nodded, her eyes filled with a quiet resolve. "My grandmother always said there were stories that needed to be told. I'm with you, whatever it takes."

Mr. Lee leaned forward, his expression thoughtful. "I've been researching the town's history for years, and I've always suspected there was more to the riot than what we've been told. I'll help in any way I can."

Sarah offered a reassuring smile. "And I'll work to incorporate what we learn into the school's curriculum. The next generation deserves to know the truth."

With their allies assembled, James and Nikki felt a renewed sense of hope. Together, they formulated a plan to uncover the full truth and bring peace to the spirits that lingered in Ravenswood.

Their first step was to delve deeper into the town's archives, seeking evidence of the events that had been hidden away for so long. Mr. Lee had access to a wealth of historical documents, and with his help, they began to piece together a narrative that had been obscured by time and fear.

The group gathered at the library, their eyes scanning row upon row of dusty volumes and yellowed papers. Each document was a potential key to unlocking the mysteries of the past, and they worked tirelessly to uncover the threads that connected them.

As they sifted through the materials, they discovered letters exchanged between town officials, minutes from secret meetings, and accounts from witnesses who had been too afraid to speak out. The picture that emerged was one of betrayal and conspiracy, a concerted effort to suppress the truth and maintain the status quo.

One letter, in particular, caught James's attention. It was from the town's mayor at the time, addressed to an outside party. The language was cryptic, but it hinted at a deal made to cover up the events of the riot in exchange for political and financial gain.

"This is it," James murmured, his heart racing with the implications. "This is the proof we've been looking for."

The group exchanged glances, the weight of their discoveries settling over them like a shroud. They knew they had to proceed carefully, aware of the potential consequences of their actions.

With the evidence in hand, James and Nikki knew they needed to expand their coalition of allies. The truth they had uncovered was powerful, but it would take the collective will of the community to bring it to light and seek justice for the past.

They decided to hold another meeting, this time inviting a wider circle of residents who might be open to their message. Maya helped spread the word, reaching out to those who had expressed interest in learning more about the town's history.

The meeting was held at the community center, the same location where the previous gathering had been disrupted by supernatural occurrences. This time, however, the atmosphere was one of cautious optimism, a sense that the town was ready to confront its past and forge a new path forward.

As people filed into the room, James and Nikki felt a flicker of hope. The turnout was larger than they had anticipated, with a diverse group of residents spanning generations. Some faces were familiar, while others were new, but all shared a common curiosity about the truth that had remained hidden for so long.

Nikki opened the meeting, her voice clear and confident. "Thank you all for coming. We've gathered more evidence about the events of the race riot and the cover-up that followed. We believe it's time for Ravenswood to face its history and seek justice for those who have been silenced."

James continued, his tone earnest. "We know this won't be easy, and there will be resistance. But we have the power to change the narrative, to bring healing and reconciliation to our community."

As they shared their findings, the room was filled with a mix of reactions—shock, disbelief, and a growing determination to uncover the truth. The evidence they presented was compelling, and the townspeople listened intently, their expressions shifting from skepticism to understanding.

Maya spoke next, her passion evident in every word. "This is about more than just uncovering the past. It's about making sure something like this never happens again. We have a responsibility to honor those who came before us and to create a better future for the next generation."

Her words resonated with the audience, and as the meeting progressed, a sense of solidarity began to take hold. The townspeople were beginning to see the power of collective action, the potential for change that lay within their grasp.

Despite the progress they were making, James and Nikki knew that not everyone was supportive of their efforts. There were those who had a vested interest in maintaining the status quo, who saw their actions as a threat to their power and influence.

Among their adversaries were members of the town council, individuals who had long benefited from the silence surrounding the riot and its aftermath. These power brokers were determined to protect their secrets, and they viewed the couple's investigation as an unwelcome intrusion.

In the days following the meeting, James and Nikki began to feel the weight of opposition bearing down on them. They received veiled warnings and hostile glares, subtle reminders that their presence was not welcome. It was clear that the stakes were high, and the path ahead would be fraught with challenges.

One afternoon, as they walked through the town square, they were approached by a man they recognized as a member of the council. His expression was one of thinly veiled contempt, his voice dripping with condescension.

"You two are stirring up trouble," he said, his tone sharp. "Some things are better left buried."

James met his gaze, his resolve unwavering. "We're not here to cause trouble. We're here to uncover the truth and bring justice to those who have been wronged."

The man's eyes narrowed, his posture tense. "Be careful," he warned. "Some people won't take kindly to outsiders meddling in their affairs."

As he walked away, Nikki felt a chill skitter down her spine. The encounter was a stark reminder of the forces arrayed against them, the lengths to which some would go to protect their secrets.

Undeterred by the opposition, James and Nikki pressed on, determined to see their mission through to the end. With the support of their growing coalition, they began to formulate a plan to bring the truth to light and honor the voices of the past.

Their first step was to organize a public event—a memorial service for the victims of the riot, a chance for the community to come together and acknowledge the pain and suffering that had been hidden for so long. The service would be held at the site of the riot, a place that had long been shrouded in silence and mystery.

Maya took charge of the logistics, coordinating with local organizations and securing the necessary permits. Sarah worked to engage the schools, encouraging students to participate and learn about the history of their town. Mrs. Jensen and Mr. Lee reached out to older residents, inviting them to share their stories and memories of the events that had shaped their lives.

As the plans took shape, James and Nikki felt a renewed sense of purpose. The memorial service would be a powerful statement of solidarity, a chance for the town to confront its past and begin the process of healing and reconciliation.

As the day of the memorial service approached, the town was abuzz with anticipation. The events of the past weeks had sparked conversations and debates, with residents grappling with the complex history that had been unearthed.

On the morning of the service, the sky was overcast, a gentle breeze rustling the leaves of the trees that lined the streets. James and Nikki arrived early, their hearts filled with a mixture of nerves and hope. They were joined by Maya, Sarah, and the rest of their allies, each one a vital part of the coalition they had built.

The site of the riot had been transformed into a place of reflection and remembrance. Flowers and candles adorned the ground, and a makeshift stage had been set up for speakers to address the crowd. The atmosphere was one of quiet reverence, a recognition of the solemnity of the occasion.

As people began to gather, James and Nikki watched with a sense of awe. The turnout was larger than they had imagined, with residents from all walks of life coming together to honor the victims and acknowledge the truth of what had happened.

Nikki stepped up to the podium, her voice steady as she addressed the crowd. "Thank you all for being here today. This is a moment of great significance for our town—a chance to honor those who suffered and to commit ourselves to a future of justice and reconciliation."

James joined her, his tone filled with conviction. "We stand here today not just to remember the past, but to learn from it. We have the power to change the narrative, to create a community that values truth and justice above all else."

As the service progressed, speakers shared their stories and reflections, each one a testament to the resilience and courage of those who had come before. The crowd listened with rapt attention, their expressions a mix of sorrow and determination.

The memorial service was a turning point for Ravenswood, a moment of unity and strength that resonated deeply with all who attended. As the final speaker concluded, the crowd erupted into applause—a spontaneous expression of hope and solidarity that filled the air.

James and Nikki stood together, their hands entwined, their hearts filled with gratitude and pride. They had faced adversity and opposition, but they had also found allies and friends who shared their vision for a better future.

As the crowd began to disperse, Maya approached them, her eyes shining with emotion. "We did it," she said, her voice filled with quiet triumph. "We brought the town together."

Nikki nodded, her heart swelling with gratitude. "Yes, we did. And this is just the beginning."

James placed a hand on her shoulder, offering a reassuring smile. "We've shown that change is possible, that the past doesn't have to define us."

With the success of the memorial service, the couple knew that their journey was far from over. There were still challenges to face and truths to uncover, but they were ready to meet them head-on, guided by the strength of their convictions and the support of their community.

As the sun set over Ravenswood, casting a warm glow across the town, James and Nikki felt a sense of peace and fulfillment. They had come to Ravenswood seeking to uncover the truth, and in doing so, they had found a community united in its desire for justice and healing.

Chapter 9

Descent into Darkness

As the sun dipped below the horizon, casting a deep indigo shade over Ravenswood, James and Nikki felt the weight of their mission more than ever. Despite the progress they had made, the road ahead was fraught with challenges, and the couple knew that they were about to delve deeper into the heart of darkness that enveloped the town. The success of the memorial service had sparked hope and unity among many residents, but it had also drawn the ire of those who wished to keep the town's secrets buried.

The day after the memorial service, James and Nikki awoke to a sense of foreboding. In the quiet of their room, they could almost hear the town holding its breath, waiting for the next move in the unfolding drama. The air was thick with tension, a palpable reminder of the forces that opposed their quest for truth.

As they prepared for the day, Nikki couldn't shake the feeling that they were being watched. The shadows seemed to stretch and shift, as if imbued with a life of their own. She glanced at James, who was absorbed in reviewing their notes and plans.

"Do you feel it?" Nikki asked, her voice tinged with unease. "It's like the town is waiting for something to happen."

James looked up, meeting her gaze with a steady resolve. "I feel it too. We have to be cautious. There are people who won't stop at anything to protect their secrets."

With a shared understanding of the dangers they faced, they set out to continue their investigation, determined to uncover the truth no matter the cost.

Their first stop was the general store, where they hoped to gather any new information about the town's mood and the reactions to the memorial service. As they entered, the familiar bell above the door jingled, announcing their presence.

The atmosphere inside was tense, the usual hum of conversation replaced by hushed whispers and furtive glances. James and Nikki made their way to the counter, where the store's owner, Mr. Carter, greeted them with a nod.

"Morning," Mr. Carter said, his voice cautious. "Heard about the memorial. Quite the turnout."

James nodded, choosing his words carefully. "It was an important step for the town. We need to face our history if we want to move forward."

Mr. Carter glanced around, ensuring they weren't overheard. "Not everyone sees it that way. Some folks are saying you two are stirring up trouble. You should be careful."

Nikki met his gaze, understanding the underlying warning. "We appreciate the concern. We're just trying to do what's right."

Mr. Carter hesitated, then lowered his voice. "If you're looking for answers, you might want to check the woods. People say that's where the real secrets are buried."

The couple exchanged a glance, the implications of his words settling over them like a shroud. The woods had always been a place of mystery and danger, a shadowy realm where the past and present collided.

As they left the store, James and Nikki felt the weight of the town's opposition pressing down on them. The power brokers of Ravenswood—those who had long benefited from the silence surrounding the riot—were growing increasingly desperate to protect their interests.

The couple knew they were being watched, their movements tracked by those who saw them as a threat. It was a dangerous game, one that required careful planning and unwavering resolve.

Their next stop was the library, where they hoped to consult with Mrs. Harris about their findings and gather any additional information that might aid their investigation.

Inside, the library was a sanctuary of quiet and solitude, the scent of old books enveloping them as they entered. Mrs. Harris greeted them with a nod, her expression one of quiet concern.

"I'm glad you're here," Mrs. Harris said, her voice a soothing balm amidst the tension. "Things have been tense since the service. People are talking, and not all of it is friendly."

James nodded, understanding the underlying threat. "We know. But we can't stop now. Too much is at stake."

Mrs. Harris gestured to a table where she had laid out a collection of documents. "I've found some more materials that might help you. Be careful, though. You're stirring up a hornet's nest."

As they settled in to review the documents, the couple felt the weight of history pressing down on them—a reminder of the lives and stories that had been lost to time and fear.

Armed with new information and a renewed sense of determination, James and Nikki decided to follow Mr. Carter's advice and venture into the woods. The forest had long been a place of secrecy and danger, rumored to be the site of the riot and the subsequent cover-up.

The path to the woods was overgrown and treacherous, the underbrush thick with tangled vines and gnarled branches. As they made their way deeper into the forest, the air grew colder, the shadows lengthening with each step.

The trees loomed overhead, their branches twisting like skeletal fingers reaching out to ensnare them. The forest was alive with the whispers of the past, a haunting melody that threaded through the trees, urging them onward.

Nikki shivered, drawing her coat tighter around her. "It's like the forest is watching us," she murmured, her voice barely above a whisper.

James nodded, his heart pounding in his chest. "We have to keep going. The answers are here, I can feel it."

As they pressed onward, the forest seemed to close in around them, the path narrowing until it was little more than a winding trail through the undergrowth. The air was thick with tension, the weight of unseen eyes pressing down on them.

Suddenly, the forest erupted into chaos. A rustling in the underbrush, the snap of a twig, and then—an eerie silence. James and Nikki froze, their senses on high alert, as they scanned the trees for any sign of movement.

Out of the shadows emerged a figure, its form indistinct and ethereal, as if caught between two worlds. The figure glided towards them, its presence unsettling yet compelling, as if it held the key to the mysteries they sought to unravel.

Nikki reached for James's hand, her heart racing with a mix of fear and anticipation. "What is it?" she whispered, her voice trembling.

James shook his head, his gaze fixed on the apparition. "I don't know. But I think it wants to show us something."

The figure beckoned to them, its gestures fluid and graceful, as it led them deeper into the heart of the forest. The couple followed, their footsteps silent on the moss-covered ground, as they ventured into the unknown.

As they reached a clearing, the figure paused, its form shimmering in the dappled sunlight that filtered through the trees. Before them lay the remnants of a gathering—a circle of stones, charred and blackened, as if scorched by fire.

The air was thick with the scent of smoke and ash, a haunting reminder of the violence that had once consumed the town. James and Nikki exchanged a glance, their shared understanding echoing between them.

"This is it," James murmured, his voice filled with awe. "This is where it happened."

Nikki nodded, her heart aching with the weight of the past. "The riot... and the cover-up. It's all here."

As they stood in the clearing, the spirits of the past seemed to surround them, their whispers threading through the air like a ghostly chorus. The couple could feel the weight of their suffering, the pain and injustice that had been hidden for so long.

The apparition, its form flickering like a candle in the wind, gestured towards the stones, urging them to listen, to understand. James and Nikki knelt, their fingers tracing the grooves etched into the stone, as they sought to connect with the memories of those who had come before.

In the silence of the forest, they heard it—a low, mournful wail that seemed to rise from the very earth, a lament for the lives lost and the stories untold. It was a sound that resonated deep within their souls, a reminder of the power of memory and the importance of truth.

As the wail subsided, the apparition turned to face them, its eyes glowing with an intensity that defied explanation. It extended a hand, its gesture one of both hope and desperation, as if pleading for their help.

James met its gaze, his resolve unwavering. "We understand. We'll do whatever it takes to bring the truth to light."

Nikki nodded, her heart swelling with determination. "We won't let your stories be forgotten. We'll fight for justice, for all of you."

With a final gesture, the apparition vanished, leaving behind an empty clearing and a renewed sense of purpose. The couple knew that their journey was far from over, but they were more determined than ever to see it through to the end.

As they made their way back through the forest, James and Nikki felt the weight of their mission pressing down on them. The path ahead would be fraught with danger and opposition, but they were resolved to face it with courage and conviction.

The power brokers of Ravenswood would not give up their secrets easily, and the couple knew they would have to navigate a treacherous web of lies and deceit to uncover the truth. But with the spirits' guidance and the support of their allies, they were determined to succeed.

As they emerged from the woods, the sun had begun to set, casting the town in a warm, golden glow. The air was filled with a sense of possibility, a promise of change that lingered on the breeze.

James and Nikki knew that the cost of truth would be high, but they were willing to pay it. For in the heart of darkness lay the promise of light, and they were resolved to bring it forth, no matter the cost.

Returning to the bed and breakfast, the couple reflected on the day's events and the path that lay ahead. The town was on the brink of transformation, its secrets on the verge of being revealed, and they were committed to leading the charge.

With each new revelation, they drew closer to understanding the full scope of Ravenswood's history and the forces that sought to keep it hidden. The journey would be long and challenging, but they were ready to face it together, guided by the strength of their convictions and the support of their community.

As they settled in for the night, James and Nikki felt a sense of peace and fulfillment. They had come to Ravenswood seeking to uncover the truth, and in doing so, they had found a community united in its desire for justice and healing.

Chapter 10

The Lost Voices

As the first light of dawn crept into their room, James and Nikki awoke with a solemn resolve. The haunting memories of their encounter in the woods lingered, a constant reminder of the spirits' urgent plea for justice. They knew they had to take their investigation to the next level, to reach out and truly understand the voices of those long silenced. It was time to bridge the gap between worlds, to seek guidance from the spirits themselves.

The idea of conducting a séance had been suggested by Maya, who had recently become a fervent supporter of their cause and a close ally. She believed that communicating directly with the spirits might provide the clarity and direction they needed to uncover the full truth about the riot and its cover-up. Initially skeptical, James and Nikki had come to realize that the supernatural occurrences they had witnessed were too significant to ignore.

They decided to hold the séance in the town's old church, a place imbued with history and a sense of reverence. Though no longer in regular use, the church remained a symbol of the community's resilience and faith. Its stone walls and stained-glass windows seemed to whisper tales of the past, inviting them to listen and learn.

Maya, who had some experience with spiritual practices, agreed to lead the séance. She gathered the necessary items—a circle of candles, a small table, and a collection of objects that had belonged to the riot victims, borrowed from the town's archives. These personal artifacts were vital, serving as conduits for the spirits' energy and memories.

As the sun began its descent, casting long shadows across the town, James and Nikki prepared to meet Maya at the church. Their hearts were a mix of anticipation and trepidation, aware that they were about to venture into uncharted territory.

The evening air was cool and crisp as they approached the church, its silhouette stark against the darkening sky. The old wooden doors creaked open, revealing the dimly lit interior that exuded an atmosphere of solemnity and peace. Maya was already there, arranging the candles in a circle at the center of the nave.

"Are you ready?" she asked, her voice calm and reassuring.

James nodded, though his heart raced with a mixture of fear and determination. "As ready as we'll ever be."

Nikki took a deep breath, steeling herself for what was to come. "We have to do this. For the spirits, and for the truth."

As the three of them settled into the circle, the candles flickered to life, casting a warm glow that danced across the pews and stained-glass windows. The air was thick with anticipation, the silence broken only by the faint rustle of leaves outside.

Maya began the séance with a prayer, her voice a gentle murmur that echoed through the church. She called upon the spirits of those who had perished in the riot, inviting them to join their circle and share their stories. Her tone was respectful and sincere, a testament to her deep connection with the spiritual realm.

As she spoke, James and Nikki closed their eyes, focusing on the energy that seemed to pulse through the room. They could feel the presence of something otherworldly, a subtle shift in the atmosphere that signaled the arrival of the spirits.

Maya's voice continued, guiding them deeper into the séance. "We are here to listen, to understand. We seek your guidance and wisdom, to help us uncover the truth and bring justice to those who have been silenced."

The air grew colder, a tangible chill that sent shivers skittering across their skin. The candles flickered wildly, their flames dancing as if caught in an unseen wind. James and Nikki exchanged a glance, their shared determination reflected in each other's eyes.

Slowly, the room began to fill with whispers—a chorus of voices that seemed to rise from the very walls. The sound was both haunting and beautiful, a melody of sorrow and longing that resonated deep within their souls.

Nikki felt a tingling sensation spread through her fingertips, as if an invisible hand was reaching out to her. She focused on the feeling, allowing it to guide her as she opened her mind to the spirits' messages.

Images flashed before her eyes—vivid and fragmented scenes of the riot, each one a glimpse into the past. She saw faces twisted in fear and anger, heard the echo of shouts and screams, felt the heat of flames that consumed everything in their path.

James experienced a similar onslaught of sensations, each one a testament to the spirits' pain and desperation. He could feel their anger, their frustration at being silenced for so long, and their determination to see justice done.

The voices grew stronger, more insistent, as if urging them to understand the full scope of the tragedy that had unfolded. It was a cacophony of emotion, a torrent of memories that flooded their senses and left them breathless.

Amidst the chaos, one voice rose above the rest—a clear, resonant tone that seemed to cut through the noise and speak directly to their hearts. It was a voice filled with both sorrow and hope, a beacon of clarity in the tumultuous sea of emotions.

"Listen," the voice said, its words echoing in their minds. "We have waited for this moment, for someone to hear our truth. The time has come to reveal what has been hidden, to set the record straight."

James and Nikki focused on the voice, their minds attuned to its message. They could sense the urgency behind the words, the spirits' desperate need to be heard and understood.

"The riot was not just an act of violence," the voice continued. "It was a betrayal, a conspiracy orchestrated by those in power to maintain control. We were used as pawns in their game, our lives sacrificed for their gain."

The revelation sent a shockwave through the couple, confirming their suspicions and igniting a fire of determination within them. They could feel the spirits' pain and anger, their desire to see those responsible held accountable.

"We need you to be our voice," the spirit implored. "To carry our story to the world, to demand justice and recognition for what we endured. Only then can we find peace."

As the voice faded, the room was filled with a profound silence, a stillness that settled over them like a gentle embrace. The candles burned steadily, their flames casting a warm glow that illuminated the circle.

Maya opened her eyes, her expression one of awe and reverence. "They've entrusted us with their truth," she said, her voice filled with emotion. "We have to honor their stories and fight for justice."

James and Nikki nodded, their hearts filled with a renewed sense of purpose. They knew that the path ahead would be challenging, but they were ready to face it with courage and conviction.

As the séance concluded, the trio remained seated in the circle, reflecting on the messages they had received. The spirits had entrusted them with a sacred duty, one that required both strength and resilience.

"We have to confront those responsible," James said, his voice steady despite the weight of their task. "We can't let them hide behind lies and deceit any longer."

Nikki agreed, her resolve unwavering. "The town deserves to know the truth, and the spirits deserve justice. We have to be their voice, to carry their message to the world."

Maya placed a reassuring hand on their shoulders. "You're not alone in this. We'll stand with you, every step of the way."

The séance had given them the clarity and direction they needed, a roadmap to guide them through the challenges that lay ahead. Armed with the spirits' messages, James and Nikki were determined to confront the town's power brokers and demand accountability for the cover-up that had kept the truth hidden for so long.

As they left the church, the night air was filled with a sense of promise and possibility. The spirits' voices still echoed in their minds, a constant reminder of the importance of their mission.

The path to justice would be fraught with danger and opposition, but they were resolved to see it through to the end. For in the heart of darkness lay the promise of light, and they were determined to bring it forth, no matter the cost.

Returning to the bed and breakfast, James and Nikki felt a renewed sense of hope and determination. The town was on the brink of transformation, its secrets poised to be revealed, and they were committed to leading the charge.

With each new revelation, they drew closer to understanding the full scope of Ravenswood's history and the forces that sought to keep it hidden. The journey would be long and challenging, but they were ready to face it together, guided by the strength of their convictions and the support of their community.

As they settled in for the night, they knew that the power of unity and the strength of community would guide them on their path, bringing hope and healing to a town long haunted by its history.

Together, they would continue their quest to honor the voices of the past, to bring light to the shadows that had lingered for far too long. The journey ahead would be challenging, but they were determined to see it through to the end.

Chapter 11

The Reckoning

As dawn broke over Ravenswood, the air was thick with anticipation and the promise of a new beginning. James and Nikki awoke with a renewed sense of purpose, their hearts bolstered by the messages they had received during the séance. The spirits had entrusted them with a sacred duty: to confront those responsible for the cover-up and demand accountability for the injustices that had plagued the town for so long. Today, they would face the town's power brokers, armed with the truth and the courage to reveal it.

Their first task was to gather their allies, those who had stood by them throughout their journey and shared their vision for justice and reconciliation. Maya, with her unwavering determination and passion for truth, was already at the helm, coordinating with other supporters to ensure that their voices would be heard.

As the morning sun cast its golden glow across the town, James and Nikki met with Maya, Sarah, Mr. Lee, and other key allies at the community center. The atmosphere was charged with a mix of apprehension and resolve, each person acutely aware of the significance of the day.

"We've come a long way," Nikki began, her voice steady despite the weight of their mission. "Today, we confront those who've kept the town in the dark for too long. We're not just doing this for the spirits, but for everyone in Ravenswood."

Maya nodded, her eyes shining with determination. "We've uncovered the truth, and now it's time to make sure it's known. We have the support of the community, and together, we can demand change."

Mr. Lee, the local historian, spoke up next. "The evidence we've gathered is compelling. It's time to hold the power brokers accountable for their actions. We owe it to the victims and to future generations."

With a shared sense of purpose, the group finalized their plans. They would present their findings at a town hall meeting later that day, ensuring that the entire community would bear witness to the revelations.

The town hall, a stately building that had stood at the heart of Ravenswood for over a century, was abuzz with activity as the time for the meeting approached. Residents from all walks of life gathered, their expressions a mix of curiosity, skepticism, and hope. The events of recent weeks had stirred emotions and sparked conversations, and now, the town was poised on the brink of transformation.

Inside, the atmosphere was electric, the air crackling with anticipation. James and Nikki took their places at the front of the room, their hearts pounding with a mixture of nerves and determination. The room filled quickly, with standing room only as townspeople crowded in to hear the truth that had been hidden for so long.

As the meeting began, the mayor called the assembly to order, his demeanor one of cautious authority. He was a man who had long been a fixture in the town's political landscape, his influence extending into every corner of the community. Yet today, his usual air of confidence seemed tinged with unease.

Nikki was the first to speak, her voice clear and unwavering. "Thank you all for coming. We're here today to discuss the events surrounding the race riot and the subsequent cover-up that has kept the truth hidden for far too long."

James stepped forward, holding up a folder filled with documents. "We've uncovered evidence that points to a conspiracy orchestrated by those in power—a cover-up designed to protect their interests at the expense of justice and truth."

As James and Nikki began to present their findings, the tension in the room was palpable. They displayed documents and photographs on a projector screen, each piece of evidence a damning testament to the lengths to which the town's leaders had gone to suppress the truth.

The crowd watched in stunned silence as the couple laid out the details of their investigation, tracing the web of deceit and betrayal that had ensnared Ravenswood for generations. The evidence was irrefutable, a stark reminder of the pain and suffering that had been hidden beneath a veneer of normalcy.

Gasps and murmurs rippled through the audience as the revelations unfolded, the weight of the truth settling over them like a shroud. For many, it was a moment of awakening—a realization that the town they had called home was built on a foundation of lies and secrets.

Maya took the floor next, her passion evident in every word. "This is about more than just uncovering the past. It's about acknowledging the pain and injustice that have been inflicted and working towards a future of healing and reconciliation."

Her words resonated with the crowd, their expressions shifting from shock to determination. The townspeople were beginning to see the power of collective action, the potential for change that lay within their grasp.

As the presentation drew to a close, the atmosphere in the room had shifted. There was a sense of urgency and resolve, a collective understanding that the time for complacency was over. It was a moment of reckoning, a chance for the town to confront its history and demand accountability from those who had perpetuated the cover-up.

The mayor, his usual composure shaken, rose to address the assembly. His voice was measured, though his eyes betrayed a flicker of uncertainty. "These are serious accusations," he began, his tone cautious. "If they are true, we must address them. But we must also proceed with care, ensuring that we do not undermine the fabric of our community."

James met the mayor's gaze, his resolve unwavering. "The fabric of our community is already torn, held together by lies and silence. It's time to mend it with truth and justice."

Nikki nodded in agreement, her heart swelling with determination. "We can't move forward if we're shackled to the past. We have to confront the truth, no matter how painful, and work towards a better future."

As the mayor considered their words, a ripple of agreement spread through the crowd. The townspeople were ready for change, willing to face the difficult truths that had been hidden for so long.

Despite the mounting pressure, there were those in the room who remained resistant—individuals who had long benefited from the status quo and saw the couple's investigation as a threat to their power and influence.

One such figure, a prominent businessman with deep ties to the town's leadership, rose to speak. His expression was one of thinly veiled contempt, his voice dripping with condescension. "These are serious accusations, but we must be cautious. We cannot allow outsiders to dictate our history and disrupt our community."

His words were met with a murmur of agreement from a few corners of the room, a reminder that the path to justice would not be without opposition.

Nikki met the businessman's gaze, her resolve unwavering. "We're not here to dictate history. We're here to uncover the truth and ensure that the voices of those who were silenced are finally heard."

Maya, her eyes filled with determination, added her voice to the chorus. "This is about justice, about creating a future where we can all thrive. We owe it to the victims, to ourselves, and to future generations."

As the debate continued, it became clear that the tide was turning. The townspeople were beginning to see the power of unity, the strength that came from standing together in pursuit of a common goal. The evidence was compelling, and the call for accountability was growing louder with each passing moment.

Sarah, the schoolteacher, rose to speak, her voice steady and filled with conviction. "We have an opportunity to teach our children the value of truth and justice, to show them that we can learn from our mistakes and build a better future."

Her words resonated with the crowd, a reminder of the importance of education and the potential for change that lay within their grasp.

Throughout the meeting, the spirits of those who had perished in the riot seemed to linger, their presence a constant reminder of the importance of their mission. James and Nikki could feel their energy, a guiding force that urged them to continue their quest for justice.

The séance had given them the clarity and direction they needed, a roadmap to guide them through the challenges that lay ahead. Armed with the spirits' messages, they were determined to confront the town's power brokers and demand accountability for the cover-up that had kept the truth hidden for so long.

As the meeting drew to a close, the mood in the room was one of hope and determination. The townspeople were ready to confront their history, to demand change and work towards a future of healing and reconciliation.

James and Nikki stood together, their hearts filled with gratitude and pride. They had faced adversity and opposition, but they had also found allies and friends who shared their vision for a better future.

As the townspeople filed out of the hall, the couple felt a renewed sense of purpose. The path to justice would be fraught with challenges, but they were resolved to see it through to the end.

For in the heart of darkness lay the promise of light, and they were determined to bring it forth, no matter the cost. As they looked to the future, they knew that the power of unity and the strength of community would guide them on their path, bringing hope and healing to a town long haunted by its history.

As the sun set over Ravenswood, casting a warm glow across the town, James and Nikki felt a sense of peace and fulfillment. They had come to Ravenswood seeking to uncover the truth, and in doing so, they had found a community united in its desire for justice and healing.

Together with their allies, they would continue their quest to honor the voices of the past, to bring light to the shadows that had lingered for far too long. The journey ahead would be challenging, but they were determined to see it through to the end.

For in the heart of darkness lay the promise of light, and they were resolved to bring it forth, no matter the cost. As they looked to the future, they knew that the spirits' guidance and their own unwavering resolve would lead them to the truth and justice they sought.

With the power of unity and the strength of community behind them, James and Nikki were ready to face whatever challenges lay ahead, confident in the knowledge that they were not alone in their quest for truth and justice. The town of Ravenswood was on the brink of transformation, and they were committed to leading the charge, bringing hope and healing to a community long haunted by its history.

Chapter 12

The Final Stand

As the day of reckoning dawned over Ravenswood, the town lay under a heavy blanket of anticipation. The air was charged with an electrifying tension, as if the very fabric of the town was holding its breath, waiting for the truth to be laid bare. James and Nikki awoke with a sense of urgency and purpose, their mission clear: they would confront the past and demand justice for the spirits who had been silenced for so long.

The events of the past weeks had led to this moment—a culmination of supernatural occurrences, hidden truths, and a community struggling to come to terms with its history. The spirits of those who had perished in the riot were growing more restless, their presence almost tangible in the early morning light. They had entrusted James and Nikki with their stories, their pain, and their desire for justice. Now, it was up to the living to decide whether to heed their call or face the consequences of continued denial.

As the couple prepared for the day, a palpable sense of determination settled over them. They knew that this was their final stand, a chance to fulfill the promise they had made to the spirits and to themselves. The town's legacy hung in the balance, and they were resolved to see it through, no matter the cost.

The town square, a place steeped in both history and mystery, had been chosen as the site for the climactic event. It was here that the riot had erupted all those years ago, and it was here that the truth would finally be revealed. The square was a symbol of Ravenswood's past, a reminder of the pain and suffering that had been hidden beneath a veneer of normalcy.

As the sun rose higher in the sky, casting its golden light across the town, residents began to gather at the square. The atmosphere was a mix of curiosity, anxiety, and hope—a community on the brink of transformation. The events of recent days had sparked conversations and debates, and now, the people of Ravenswood were ready to confront their history and decide their future.

James and Nikki arrived early, their hearts pounding with a mixture of nerves and determination. They were joined by Maya, Sarah, Mr. Lee, and other key allies, each one a vital part of the coalition they had built. Together, they had uncovered the truth and rallied the community to demand change. Now, they stood united, ready to face whatever challenges lay ahead.

As the crowd swelled, the air grew thick with anticipation. The spirits, ever-present and unyielding, seemed to hover at the edges of the square, their energy palpable to those attuned to their presence. James and Nikki could feel their urgency, a silent plea for recognition and justice.

Maya, who had become a trusted leader in the movement, stepped forward to address the crowd. Her voice was clear and confident, carrying the weight of their collective mission. "Thank you all for being here today. We stand together at a pivotal moment in our town's history—a chance to confront the past and choose a path toward healing and reconciliation."

Her words resonated with the crowd, a reminder of the importance of unity and courage. The townspeople listened intently, their expressions a mix of hope and trepidation. They knew that the truth, once revealed, could not be ignored, and they were prepared to face the consequences of their actions.

James and Nikki took their places at the front of the gathering, their hearts filled with a sense of purpose and resolve. They knew that the evidence they had uncovered was powerful—a testament to the lengths to which the town's leaders had gone to suppress the truth. Today, they would present their findings and demand accountability from those who had perpetuated the cover-up.

As the couple began to speak, the atmosphere in the square was electric, the air crackling with anticipation. They laid out the details of their investigation, tracing the web of deceit and betrayal that had ensnared Ravenswood for generations. The evidence was irrefutable, a stark reminder of the pain and suffering that had been hidden beneath a veneer of normalcy.

Gasps and murmurs rippled through the crowd as the revelations unfolded, the weight of the truth settling over them like a shroud. For many, it was a moment of awakening—a realization that the town they had called home was built on a foundation of lies and secrets.

As the presentation continued, the spirits made their presence known in a powerful and undeniable way. The air grew colder, a tangible chill that sent shivers skittering across the skin of those gathered. The candles placed around the square flickered wildly, their flames dancing as if caught in an unseen wind.

A low, mournful wail echoed through the square, a haunting melody that seemed to rise from the very earth. It was a sound that resonated deep within the souls of those present, a reminder of the power of memory and the importance of truth.

The spirits, emboldened by the presence of those who sought justice, seemed to demand acknowledgment and action. Their whispers threaded through the crowd, urging them to listen, to understand, and to act.

As the spirits' presence intensified, the townspeople were faced with a choice: to acknowledge their history and seek redemption, or to continue living in denial and face the wrath of those they had wronged. It was a moment of reckoning, a chance for Ravenswood to confront its legacy and decide its future.

The mayor, who had long been a fixture in the town's political landscape, rose to address the assembly. His usual air of confidence was shaken, his voice tinged with uncertainty. "These revelations are difficult to hear, but they are necessary. We must confront our past if we are to build a future of healing and reconciliation."

His words were met with a murmur of agreement from the crowd, a reminder that the path to justice required both courage and accountability. The townspeople were beginning to see the power of unity, the strength that came from standing together in pursuit of a common goal.

As the debate continued, it became clear that the tide was turning. The townspeople were ready to confront their history, to demand change and work towards a future of healing and reconciliation. The evidence was compelling, and the call for accountability was growing louder with each passing moment.

Sarah, the schoolteacher, rose to speak, her voice steady and filled with conviction. "We have an opportunity to teach our children the value of truth and justice, to show them that we can learn from our mistakes and build a better future."

Her words resonated with the crowd, a reminder of the importance of education and the potential for change that lay within their grasp.

As the meeting drew to a close, the mood in the square was one of hope and determination. The townspeople were ready to confront their history, to demand change and work towards a future of healing and reconciliation. The spirits, their presence a constant reminder of the importance of their mission, seemed to offer their blessing—a promise that justice and recognition were within reach.

James and Nikki stood together, their hearts filled with gratitude and pride. They had faced adversity and opposition, but they had also found allies and friends who shared their vision for a better future.

As the townspeople filed out of the square, the couple felt a renewed sense of purpose. The path to justice would be fraught with challenges, but they were resolved to see it through to the end.

As the sun set over Ravenswood, casting a warm glow across the town, James and Nikki felt a sense of peace and fulfillment. They had come to Ravenswood seeking to uncover the truth, and in doing so, they had found a community united in its desire for justice and healing.

Together with their allies, they would continue their quest to honor the voices of the past, to bring light to the shadows that had lingered for far too long. The journey ahead would be challenging, but they were determined to see it through to the end.

For in the heart of darkness lay the promise of light, and they were resolved to bring it forth, no matter the cost. As they looked to the future, they knew that the spirits' guidance and their own unwavering resolve would lead them to the truth and justice they sought.

With the power of unity and the strength of community behind them, James and Nikki were ready to face whatever challenges lay ahead, confident in the knowledge that they were not alone in their quest for truth and justice. The town of Ravenswood was on the brink of transformation, and they were committed to leading the charge, bringing hope and healing to a community long haunted by its history.

As the night enveloped Ravenswood, the town lay beneath a canopy of stars, its future filled with promise and possibility. The events of the day had marked a turning point, a moment of reckoning that had set the stage for a new beginning.

James and Nikki reflected on their journey, their hearts filled with gratitude for the support and solidarity they had found in the community. They knew that the path to justice was long and challenging, but they were ready to face it with courage and conviction.

As they prepared to leave the square, the spirits' presence lingered, a gentle reminder of the power of memory and the importance of truth. They had entrusted James and Nikki with their stories, their pain, and their desire for justice. Now, the couple was resolved to honor that trust, to carry their message to the world, and to ensure that their voices would never be silenced again.

With a renewed sense of purpose and a commitment to change, James and Nikki looked to the future, confident in the knowledge that they were part of a community united in its desire for healing and reconciliation. Together, they would continue their quest to bring light to the shadows, to create a brighter future for all, and to honor the voices of the past.

For in the heart of darkness lay the promise of light, and they were resolved to bring it forth, no matter the cost. As they looked to the future, they knew that the spirits' guidance and their own unwavering resolve would lead them to the truth and justice they sought.

Chapter 13

A New Dawn

As the first light of dawn crept over Ravenswood, the town stirred with a newfound sense of purpose and hope. The previous day's events had marked a turning point—a reckoning that had set the stage for healing and reconciliation. James and Nikki awoke to the sound of birdsong filtering through their window, a gentle reminder of the promise of a new beginning.

The air was crisp and invigorating, filled with the scent of fresh earth and the warmth of the sun's early rays. As they dressed and prepared to face the day, James and Nikki felt a sense of peace and fulfillment, their hearts buoyed by the knowledge that they had played a part in bringing the truth to light.

The town square, once a place shrouded in silence and mystery, had become a vibrant hub of activity and transformation. The events of recent weeks had sparked conversations and debates, encouraging residents from all walks of life to come together in pursuit of a common goal: to honor the past and build a brighter future.

As the sun rose higher in the sky, casting its golden glow across the town, residents began to gather in the square for a memorial service dedicated to the victims of the riot. The atmosphere was one of reverence and reflection, a recognition of the solemnity of the occasion.

James and Nikki arrived early, their hearts filled with a mix of anticipation and gratitude. They were joined by Maya, Sarah, Mr. Lee, and other key allies who had supported them throughout their journey. Together, they had uncovered the truth and rallied the community to demand change. Now, they stood united, ready to celebrate the progress they had made and to honor those who had come before.

The square was adorned with flowers and candles, each one a symbol of remembrance and hope. A makeshift stage had been set up for speakers to address the crowd, and a plaque bearing the names of the riot victims had been installed as a permanent tribute to their memory.

As the crowd swelled, the air was filled with a sense of unity and purpose. People of all ages and backgrounds had come together to honor the past and to commit themselves to a future of healing and reconciliation. The memorial service was a testament to the power of community—a reminder that, despite the challenges they faced, the people of Ravenswood were willing to confront their history and work towards a better future.

Maya, who had become a trusted leader in the movement, stepped forward to open the service. Her voice was clear and confident, carrying the weight of their collective mission. "Thank you all for being here today. We gather to honor the memory of those who suffered and to commit ourselves to a future of justice and reconciliation."

Her words resonated with the crowd, a reminder of the importance of unity and courage. The townspeople listened intently, their expressions a mix of hope and determination. They knew that the truth, once revealed, could not be ignored, and they were prepared to face the consequences of their actions.

As the service continued, speakers shared their reflections and memories, each one a testament to the resilience and courage of those who had come before. The crowd listened with rapt attention, their expressions shifting from sorrow to hope as they absorbed the stories of the past.

Sarah, the schoolteacher who had become a vocal advocate for change, took the stage next. Her voice was steady and filled with conviction as she addressed the crowd. "We have an opportunity to teach our children the value of truth and justice, to show them that we can learn from our mistakes and build a better future."

Her words resonated deeply with those gathered, a reminder of the importance of education and the potential for change that lay within their grasp. The townspeople were beginning to see the power of unity, the strength that came from standing together in pursuit of a common goal.

As the service drew to a close, James and Nikki felt a renewed sense of purpose and fulfillment. They had come to Ravenswood seeking to uncover the truth, and in doing so, they had found a community united in its desire for justice and healing.

With the power of unity and the strength of community behind them, the town was poised to embark on a journey of transformation. Initiatives to educate and memorialize the past were already being put in place, ensuring that the lessons of history would not be forgotten.

One such initiative was the establishment of a permanent exhibit at the local museum, dedicated to the history of the riot and the events that had shaped Ravenswood. Curated by Mr. Lee, the exhibit featured photographs, documents, and personal artifacts that told the stories of those who had lived through the tumultuous events of the past.

The exhibit was designed to be both educational and thought-provoking, encouraging visitors to reflect on the importance of truth and justice in shaping a community's future. It was a testament to the resilience of the human spirit and a reminder that, despite the challenges they faced, the people of Ravenswood were committed to building a brighter future.

In addition to the museum exhibit, the town's schools had implemented a new curriculum focused on local history and social justice. Led by Sarah, the curriculum aimed to teach students about the importance of empathy, understanding, and the power of collective action. Through lessons and activities, students were encouraged to think critically about the past and to consider their role in shaping the future.

As the town embraced these initiatives, a sense of renewal and hope began to take hold. The events of recent weeks had brought about a transformation, not just in the physical landscape of Ravenswood, but in the hearts and minds of its residents.

People who had once been divided by fear and mistrust were now united in their desire for change. Conversations that had once been fraught with tension were now filled with understanding and empathy. The town was slowly healing, its wounds beginning to mend as the truth was finally acknowledged and embraced.

James and Nikki watched with a sense of pride and fulfillment as the town they had come to love began to blossom into a beacon of hope and change. They had played a part in this transformation, and they were grateful for the opportunity to have been a part of such a remarkable journey.

As the day wore on, the sun began its descent, casting a warm glow across the town. James and Nikki took a moment to reflect on their journey, their hearts filled with gratitude for the support and solidarity they had found in the community.

They knew that the path to justice was long and challenging, but they were ready to face it with courage and conviction. Together with their allies, they would continue their quest to honor the voices of the past, to bring light to the shadows that had lingered for far too long.

For in the heart of darkness lay the promise of light, and they were resolved to bring it forth, no matter the cost. As they looked to the future, they knew that the spirits' guidance and their own unwavering resolve would lead them to the truth and justice they sought.

With the power of unity and the strength of community behind them, James and Nikki were ready to face whatever challenges lay ahead, confident in the knowledge that they were not alone in their quest for truth and justice. The town of Ravenswood was on the brink of transformation, and they were committed to leading the charge, bringing hope and healing to a community long haunted by its history.

As the sun set over Ravenswood, casting a warm glow across the town, James and Nikki felt a sense of peace and fulfillment. They had come to Ravenswood seeking to uncover the truth, and in doing so, they had found a community united in its desire for justice and healing.

Together with their allies, they would continue their quest to honor the voices of the past, to bring light to the shadows that had lingered for far too long. The journey ahead would be challenging, but they were determined to see it through to the end.

For in the heart of darkness lay the promise of light, and they were resolved to bring it forth, no matter the cost. As they looked to the future, they knew that the spirits' guidance and their own unwavering resolve would lead them to the truth and justice they sought.

With the power of unity and the strength of community behind them, James and Nikki were ready to face whatever challenges lay ahead, confident in the knowledge that they were not alone in their quest for truth and justice. The town of Ravenswood was on the brink of transformation, and they were committed to leading the charge, bringing hope and healing to a community long haunted by its history.

As the night enveloped Ravenswood, the town lay beneath a canopy of stars, its future filled with promise and possibility. The events of the day had marked a turning point, a moment of reckoning that had set the stage for a new beginning.

James and Nikki reflected on their journey, their hearts filled with gratitude for the support and solidarity they had found in the community. They knew that the path to justice was long and challenging, but they were ready to face it with courage and conviction.

As they prepared to leave the square, the spirits' presence lingered, a gentle reminder of the power of memory and the importance of truth. They had entrusted James and Nikki with their stories, their pain, and their desire for justice. Now, the couple was resolved to honor that trust, to carry their message to the world, and to ensure that their voices would never be silenced again.

With a renewed sense of purpose and a commitment to change, James and Nikki looked to the future, confident in the knowledge that they were part of a community united in its desire for healing and reconciliation. Together, they would continue their quest to bring light to the shadows, to create a brighter future for all, and to honor the voices of the past.

Chapter 14

Reflections and Farewells

As the morning sun rose over Ravenswood, painting the sky with hues of amber and gold, James and Nikki awoke with a mix of emotions swirling in their hearts. Today marked the end of a chapter in their lives—a journey that had tested their resolve, strengthened their bond, and left an indelible mark on the town they had come to cherish. The air was crisp and cool, carrying with it the scent of fresh beginnings and the promise of change.

They lay in bed for a moment, absorbing the quiet of the morning and reflecting on the whirlwind of events that had brought them to this point. The past weeks had been a profound journey of discovery and transformation, not just for the town of Ravenswood, but for themselves as well. They had come seeking forgotten histories, and in doing so, had unearthed stories of pain and resilience, of injustice and redemption.

James turned to Nikki, his eyes filled with a mixture of gratitude and pride. "We did it," he said softly, his voice laced with awe. "We really made a difference."

Nikki nodded, her heart swelling with emotion. "We did. And it wasn't easy, but it was worth every challenge we faced."

Their thoughts drifted back to the beginning of their journey, to the moment they had first arrived in Ravenswood, unaware of the mysteries and secrets that lay beneath its surface. The town had seemed unremarkable, a quiet place nestled in the heart of the countryside. Yet, as they had delved deeper, they had uncovered layers of history and memory, of voices that had long been silenced and stories that demanded to be told.

With a shared resolve, they rose from bed and began to pack their belongings, each item a reminder of their time in Ravenswood and the people they had come to know and love. As they worked, they reflected on the impact they had made and the legacy they would leave behind.

Their first stop of the day was the local café, a quaint establishment that had become a regular haunt during their stay. The owner, Mrs. Jenkins, greeted them with a warm smile, her eyes twinkling with a mixture of sadness and pride.

"Leaving us already?" she asked, her voice tinged with emotion.

James nodded, his heart heavy with the weight of farewell. "It's time for us to move on, but we won't forget everything this town has given us."

Nikki stepped forward, her expression sincere. "Thank you for your kindness, Mrs. Jenkins. And for believing in us."

The older woman reached across the counter, squeezing Nikki's hand with a gentle firmness. "You two have done something remarkable here. Don't ever forget that."

As they sipped their coffee, James and Nikki watched the townspeople go about their morning routines, their expressions lighter and more hopeful than when they had first arrived. The changes wrought by their efforts were palpable—a renewed sense of community and a commitment to acknowledging and learning from the past.

Their next stop was the library, where Mrs. Harris awaited them with her usual air of warmth and wisdom. The librarian had been one of their staunchest allies, a beacon of knowledge and support throughout their investigation.

"I'm going to miss you two," Mrs. Harris said, her voice filled with genuine affection. "You've brought new life to this town, and I have no doubt that your work here will continue to inspire others."

James smiled, his gratitude evident in his eyes. "We couldn't have done it without you. Your support meant the world to us."

Nikki nodded in agreement, her heart full of appreciation. "Thank you for everything, Mrs. Harris. We'll carry your spirit with us on our journey."

As they made their way through the town, James and Nikki couldn't help but marvel at the transformation that had taken place. The events of recent weeks had sparked a profound change, not just in the physical landscape of Ravenswood, but in the hearts and minds of its residents.

The school, once a place of rote learning and tradition, had embraced a new curriculum focused on local history and social justice. Led by Sarah, the passionate schoolteacher who had become a vocal advocate for change, students were encouraged to think critically about the past and to consider their role in shaping the future.

The local museum, once a quiet repository of artifacts, now featured a permanent exhibit dedicated to the history of the riot and the stories of those who had lived through its tumultuous events. Curated by Mr. Lee, the exhibit served as both an educational resource and a testament to the resilience of the human spirit.

As they walked through the town square, the site of so much pain and conflict, James and Nikki were struck by the sense of renewal that permeated the air. The square had become a place of gathering and reflection, a symbol of the town's journey towards healing and reconciliation.

Their final stop was the community center, where a small gathering of friends and allies awaited them. Maya, Sarah, Mr. Lee, and others who had supported them throughout their journey had come to bid them farewell, their expressions a mix of gratitude and sadness.

Maya, who had become a trusted leader and friend, stepped forward to speak on behalf of the group. Her voice was filled with emotion as she addressed James and Nikki. "You've done something incredible here. You've given us the courage to face our past and the strength to build a better future. We'll never forget what you've done for us."

James felt a lump form in his throat, his heart swelling with pride and gratitude. "Thank you, Maya. We couldn't have done it without all of you. This town is special, and we're honored to have been a part of its transformation."

Nikki's eyes glistened with tears as she stepped forward to embrace Maya. "We'll carry all of you with us, wherever we go. You've taught us so much about resilience and the power of community."

Mr. Lee, the wise historian who had guided them through the complexities of Ravenswood's past, offered a nod of appreciation. "You've left a legacy of change here. The stories you've uncovered will continue to inspire and educate for generations to come."

As they exchanged hugs and farewells, James and Nikki were struck by the depth of the connections they had formed. What had begun as a quest for forgotten histories had blossomed into a journey of friendship and discovery, one that would stay with them for the rest of their lives.

As they prepared to leave, the couple took one final moment to reflect on their journey. They had come to Ravenswood as outsiders, seekers of stories and truths long buried. In doing so, they had unearthed not only the town's hidden past but also the strength and resilience of its people.

The impact they had made was evident in the faces of those who had gathered to bid them farewell—a testament to the power of truth and the potential for change that lay within every community.

As they turned to leave, James and Nikki felt a sense of peace and fulfillment, their hearts buoyed by the knowledge that they had played a part in bringing about a new dawn for Ravenswood.

As they drove away from the town, the road stretched out before them, promising new stories and new challenges. The journey they had undertaken in Ravenswood had been transformative, not just for the town but for themselves as well.

They had learned the importance of listening to the voices of the past, of honoring the stories of those who had been silenced, and of working towards a future of justice and reconciliation. The lessons they had learned would guide them on their next adventure, inspiring them to continue seeking the truths that lay hidden in the shadows.

As they traveled down the winding road, James and Nikki felt a renewed sense of purpose and possibility. The journey they had begun in Ravenswood was just the beginning—a stepping stone on the path to greater understanding and discovery.

Together, they would continue to seek out the stories that needed to be told, to bring light to the shadows, and to create a brighter future for all. The road ahead was filled with promise, and they were ready to face it with courage and conviction.

As the sun set on the horizon, painting the sky with hues of pink and orange, James and Nikki looked to the future with hope and anticipation. They had come to Ravenswood seeking forgotten histories, and in doing so, had uncovered a legacy of change and transformation.

With the power of unity and the strength of community behind them, they were ready to face whatever challenges lay ahead, confident in the knowledge that they were not alone in their quest for truth and justice.

For in the heart of darkness lay the promise of light, and they were resolved to bring it forth, no matter the cost. As they looked to the future, they knew that the spirits' guidance and their own unwavering resolve would lead them to the truth and justice they sought.

Together, they would honor the voices of the past, bring light to the shadows, and create a brighter future for all. The journey ahead would be challenging, but they were determined to see it through to the end, guided by the strength of their convictions and the support of their community.

As they drove into the distance, the road unfurling before them like a ribbon of possibility, James and Nikki felt a sense of excitement and anticipation. They knew that the stories they had uncovered in Ravenswood were just the beginning—a prelude to a lifetime of adventure and discovery.

Chapter 15

Onward Journeys

As the morning sun began its ascent, casting a warm glow over the sprawling countryside, James and Nikki found themselves on the open road, the town of Ravenswood receding into the distance. The gentle hum of their car's engine was a comforting backdrop to their thoughts, a reminder of the journey they had undertaken and the adventures that lay ahead.

The events of the past weeks, filled with revelations and transformations, had left an indelible mark on their hearts. Ravenswood had been more than just a stop on their road trip; it had been a profound experience that had tested their resolve, deepened their understanding of history and justice, and strengthened their bond.

James glanced over at Nikki, who was gazing out the window, her expression thoughtful yet serene. "It's hard to believe we're leaving," he said, his voice tinged with a mixture of nostalgia and anticipation.

Nikki turned to him, her eyes reflecting the same emotions. "I know. It feels like we've been a part of something truly special, something that will stay with us forever."

They both fell silent, each lost in their own reflections. The road stretched out before them, a ribbon of possibility that promised new stories and new challenges. The world was vast and filled with mysteries waiting to be uncovered, and they felt a renewed sense of purpose and excitement for the journey ahead.

Their time in Ravenswood had been transformative, not only for the town but for themselves as well. They had arrived as seekers of forgotten histories, and in doing so, had uncovered stories of pain and resilience, of injustice and redemption. The experience had taught them the power of truth and the importance of listening to the voices of the past.

James and Nikki had learned that history was not just a series of events recorded in dusty tomes, but a living, breathing tapestry woven from the lives and experiences of those who had come before. They had come to understand the profound impact that acknowledging and honoring these stories could have on a community and on themselves.

As they drove through the picturesque landscape, the rolling hills and vibrant fields serving as a reminder of the beauty of the world, they felt a renewed appreciation for the journey they had chosen to undertake. The road was not always easy, but it was filled with opportunities for growth and discovery.

"Do you think we'll find more places like Ravenswood?" Nikki asked, her voice filled with curiosity and hope.

James smiled, his heart filled with a sense of adventure. "I hope so. There are so many stories out there, just waiting to be uncovered. And I can't imagine a better partner to share them with."

Nikki reached out and squeezed his hand, her heart swelling with gratitude and love. "Me neither. Whatever comes next, we'll face it together."

As they continued their journey, James and Nikki couldn't help but reflect on the people they had met and the friendships they had forged in Ravenswood. The town had welcomed them with open arms, and they had been inspired by the courage and resilience of its residents.

They thought of Maya, whose passion and determination had been a beacon of hope amidst the darkness. Her leadership had been instrumental in rallying the community to confront its past and work towards a brighter future.

They remembered Sarah, the dedicated schoolteacher who had embraced the challenge of educating the next generation about the importance of truth and justice. Her commitment to change had been a reminder of the power of education to transform hearts and minds.

And they thought of Mr. Lee, the wise historian who had guided them through the complexities of Ravenswood's past. His knowledge and insight had been invaluable, helping them to piece together the stories that had shaped the town's history.

Each of these individuals had played a vital role in their journey, and James and Nikki felt a deep sense of gratitude for the support and solidarity they had found in the community. Ravenswood had taught them that the power of change lay within the hands of those who were willing to stand together in pursuit of a common goal.

As the sun climbed higher in the sky, casting its golden rays across the landscape, James and Nikki felt a renewed sense of hope and anticipation for the future. The road ahead was filled with endless possibilities, and they were eager to embrace the adventures that awaited them.

They talked about the places they wanted to visit, the stories they hoped to uncover, and the impact they hoped to make in the world. Their journey was far from over, and they were excited to continue exploring the stories that lay hidden in the shadows.

"We should keep a journal," Nikki suggested, her eyes alight with excitement. "Document our travels and the stories we discover. It could be a way to share our experiences and inspire others."

James nodded, his imagination already racing with possibilities. "That's a great idea. There's so much to learn and share, and I think it would be incredible to look back on our journey and see how far we've come."

They spent the next few miles discussing their plans, their voices filled with enthusiasm and determination. The road was both a physical and metaphorical journey, a path leading them to new horizons and new understandings of themselves and the world.

As they traveled further, the landscape shifted and changed, reflecting the diversity and beauty of the world they were eager to explore. Each new vista was a reminder of the endless opportunities that lay before them, a testament to the wonder and mystery of life.

James and Nikki embraced the unknown, their hearts open to the possibilities of what lay ahead. They knew that the journey would not always be easy, but they were prepared to face whatever challenges awaited them with courage and resilience.

Their experiences in Ravenswood had taught them the importance of listening and understanding, of approaching each new place and each new story with empathy and respect. They were committed to honoring the voices of the past and to working towards a future of justice and reconciliation.

As the miles slipped by, they felt a sense of freedom and possibility that was both exhilarating and humbling. The world was vast and filled with stories waiting to be discovered, and they were ready to embrace the adventure.

As they continued their journey, James and Nikki carried with them the lessons they had learned and the impact they had made in Ravenswood. The town had been a transformative experience, one that had left an indelible mark on their hearts and minds.

They were proud of the legacy they had helped to create—a legacy of change and transformation that would continue to inspire and educate for generations to come. Ravenswood had shown them the power of unity and the strength of community, and they were determined to carry that spirit with them wherever they went.

Their journey was a testament to the importance of truth and justice, of listening to the voices of the past and working towards a brighter future. They were committed to continuing their quest, to uncovering the stories that needed to be told and to bringing light to the shadows.

As the sun began its descent, casting a warm glow across the landscape, James and Nikki felt a sense of peace and fulfillment. They had come to Ravenswood seeking forgotten histories, and in doing so, had uncovered a legacy of change and transformation.

With the power of unity and the strength of community behind them, they were ready to face whatever challenges lay ahead, confident in the knowledge that they were not alone in their quest for truth and justice.

For in the heart of darkness lay the promise of light, and they were resolved to bring it forth, no matter the cost. As they looked to the future, they knew that the spirits' guidance and their own unwavering resolve would lead them to the truth and justice they sought.

Together, they would honor the voices of the past, bring light to the shadows, and create a brighter future for all. The journey ahead would be challenging, but they were determined to see it through to the end, guided by the strength of their convictions and the support of their community.

As the stars began to twinkle in the night sky, James and Nikki felt a sense of excitement and anticipation for the journey that lay ahead. They knew that the stories they had uncovered in Ravenswood were just the beginning—a prelude to a lifetime of adventure and discovery.

With hearts full of hope and minds open to the endless possibilities of the future, they embraced the journey that lay ahead, ready to face whatever challenges awaited them with courage and conviction.

For in the heart of darkness lay the promise of light, and they were resolved to bring it forth, no matter the cost. As they looked to the future, they knew that the spirits' guidance and their own unwavering resolve would lead them to the truth and justice they sought.

Together, they would continue their quest to honor the voices of the past, to bring light to the shadows, and to create a brighter future for all. The journey ahead would be challenging, but they were determined to see it through to the end, guided by the strength of their convictions and the support of their community.

As they continued down the road, the horizon stretched out before them, promising new stories and new challenges. The world was vast and filled with mysteries waiting to be uncovered, and they felt a renewed sense of purpose and excitement for the journey ahead.

James and Nikki knew that they were part of something greater than themselves—a movement towards understanding and reconciliation, towards a future where the stories of the past were honored and the voices of the silenced were heard.

With the power of unity and the strength of community behind them, they were ready to face whatever challenges lay ahead, confident in the knowledge that they were not alone in their quest for truth and justice.

As they drove into the night, the road unfurling before them like a ribbon of possibility, James and Nikki felt a sense of excitement and anticipation. They knew that the stories they had uncovered in Ravenswood were just the beginning—a prelude to a lifetime of adventure and discovery.

With hearts full of hope and minds open to the endless possibilities of the future, they embraced the journey that lay ahead, ready to face whatever challenges awaited them with courage and conviction.

Books by Kerry Brackett

Poetry

Soul Appetizer https://shorturl.at/cLFCn

An Open Table https://shorturl.at/SPjJy

Surviving Myself https://shorturl.at/U6eU1

Journeys of the Unseen series *https://shorturl.at/8wqlz*

Shadows at Sundown

Light on the Horizon

ABOUT THE AUTHOR

Kerry Brackett received his Ed.D. in Higher Education Administration from Liberty University and his MA in English and Creative Writing from Southern New Hampshire University. He has won a National Poetry Award for Freedom Poet of the Year in 2015 and a Gifted Artist Neo-Soul and Poetry Award in 2016. His poems, short stories, and essays appear or are forthcoming in many journals and anthologies, including *The Black & Latinx Poetry Project*, *The Griot, Simply Elevate Magazine, Spoken Vizions Magazine, Inner Child Press' I Want My Poetry to... Anthology* and *Wicked Shadow Press*. His debut poetry chapbook, *Soul Appetizer,* was self-published in 2012. His second book, *An Open Table*, was released in 2013. He released his third poetry chapbook, *Surviving Myself* (Guerrilla Ignition Publishing), in 2020. He had released numerous spoken word albums, including *Kadence of a Poetic Gentleman*, which won an Akademia Music Award for Best Spoken Word Album in 2016. He currently lives in Bessemer, Alabama.

Made in the USA
Columbia, SC
09 February 2025

53266540R00067